CONTENTS

A Tale of the Secret Saint

NOVEL **3**

WRITTEN BY
Touya

ILLUSTRATED BY
chibi

Airship

Seven Seas Entertainment

Tensei Sita Daiseijyo ha, Seijyo dearuko towohitakakusu Vol.3
© Touya, chibi 2020
Originally published in Japan in 2020
by EARTH STAR Entertainment, Tokyo.
English translation rights arranged
with EARTH STAR Entertainment, Tokyo,
through TOHAN CORPORATION, Tokyo.

Seven Seas press and purchase enquiries can be sent to
Marketing Manager Lianne Sentar at press@gomanga.com.
Information regarding the distribution and purchase of
digital editions is available from Digital Manager CK Russell
at digital@gomanga.com.

Follow Seven Seas Entertainment online at
sevenseasentertainment.com.

TRANSLATION: Kevin Ishizaka
ADAPTATION: Matthew Birkenhauer
COVER DESIGN: H. Qi
LOGO DESIGN: George Panella
INTERIOR LAYOUT & DESIGN: Clay Gardner
COPY EDITOR: Meg van Huygen
PROOFREADER: Jade Gardner
LIGHT NOVEL EDITOR: Nicasio Reed
PREPRESS TECHNICIAN: Melanie Ujimori
PRINT MANAGER: Rhiannon Rasmussen-Silverstein
PRODUCTION MANAGER: Lissa Pattillo
EDITOR-IN-CHIEF: Julie Davis
ASSOCIATE PUBLISHER: Adam Arnold
PUBLISHER: Jason DeAngelis

ISBN: 978-1-63858-181-9
Printed in Canada
First Printing: July 2022
10 9 8 7 6 5 4 3 2 1

THE STORY THUS FAR

FIA, THE YOUNGEST DAUGHTER of the Ruud knight family, master of a black dragon and new recruit to the First Knight Brigade, must hide the fact that she was the Great Saint in her previous life, out of fear of the demon that killed her.

However, on her very first trip out exterminating monsters, she inadvertently draws attention to herself by showing deep knowledge of monsters that no rookie knight could ever hope to have. Because of this, she's sent to the Fourth Monster Tamer Knight Brigade, where she is made to look after the Brigade's familiars. She takes the time to call on her familiar, Zavilia, the black dragon.

But when Zavilia is spotted by her fellow Knights, a joint expedition between the Fourth and Sixth Knight Brigades is mounted to search for him. During the expedition, Fia is attacked by two blue dragons. Zavilia makes quick work of them and realizes how important Fia is to him. He then decides to leave on a journey, swearing to return to her as the ruler of all dragons, the Black Dragon King.

Náv Kingdom
CHARACTER LIST

FIA RUUD

Youngest daughter of the Ruud knight family. A princess and the Great Saint in her past life. Currently hiding her status as a saint and living as a knight...for now.

ZAVILIA

Fia's familiar. The only black dragon in the world. One of the Three Great Beasts of the continent.

SAVIZ NÁV

Commander of the Náv Black Dragon Knights. The younger brother of the king and, as such, the heir apparent.

CYRIL SUTHERLAND

Captain of the First Knight Brigade. Head of the most prominent duke family and second in line to the throne. Also known as the "Dragon of Náv." Strongest swordsman in the entirety of the Knight Brigade.

DESMOND RONAN

Captain of the Second Knight Brigade and Commandant of the Military Police. Head of an earl family. Also known as the "Tiger of Náv." Has had a thing against women ever since his younger brother ran off with his fiancée.

ZACKARY TOWNSEND

Captain of the Sixth Knight Brigade. Well liked by his subordinates. Chivalrous and caring.

KURTIS BANNISTER

Captain of the Thirteenth Knight Brigade. Former knight of the First Knight Brigade. Perhaps the weakest of the captains?

Náv Black Dragon Knight Brigade
COMMANDER: SAVIZ NÁV

	Captain	Vice-Captain	Knight
First Knight Brigade ROYAL FAMILY GUARDS	Cyril Sutherland		Fia Ruud, Fabian Wyner
Second Knight Brigade ROYAL CASTLE SECURITY	Desmond Ronan		
Third Mage Knight Brigade MAGES	Enoch		
Fourth Monster Tamer Knight Brigade MONSTER TAMERS	Quentin Agutter	Gideon Oakes	Patty
Fifth Knight Brigade ROYAL CAPITAL GUARDS	Clarissa Abernethy		
Sixth Knight Brigade MONSTER EXTERMINATION, ROYAL CASTLE VICINITY	Zackary Townsend		
Seventh Knight Brigade MONSTER EXTERMINATION, NORTH			
Eighth Knight Brigade MONSTER EXTERMINATION, EAST			
Ninth Knight Brigade MONSTER EXTERMINATION, SOUTH			
Tenth Knight Brigade MONSTER EXTERMINATION, WEST			
Eleventh Knight Brigade BORDER PATROL, FAR NORTH			
Twelfth Knight Brigade BORDER PATROL, FAR EAST			
Thirteenth Knight Brigade BORDER PATROL, FAR SOUTH	Kurtis Bannister		
Fourteenth Knight Brigade BORDER PATROL, FAR WEST		Dolph Ruud	
Fifteenth Knight Brigade BORDER PATROL			
Sixteenth Knight Brigade BORDER PATROL			
Seventeenth Knight Brigade BORDER PATROL			
Eighteenth Knight Brigade BORDER PATROL			
Nineteenth Knight Brigade BORDER PATROL			
Twentieth Knight Brigade BORDER PATROL			

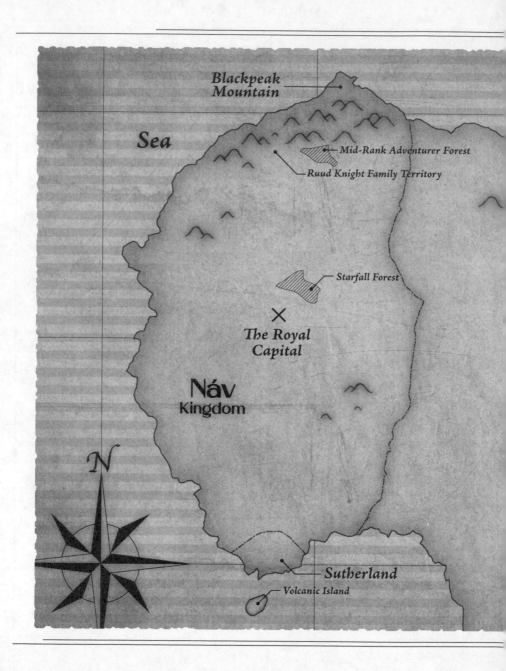

25
Return to the First Knight Brigade

THE DAY AFTER the black dragon search, I returned to the First Knight Brigade. Deep down, I really must've wanted to come back—it'd only been a few days, but I was overjoyed to see Cyril's face.

The moment I opened the door and laid eyes on him, I just had to rush right in. "Captain Cyril!" He stood up from his desk and approached, and I stopped before him to give the standard knight salute. "I, Fia Ruud, have returned to the First Knight Brigade!"

"Welcome back, Fia," he said tenderly. He was smiling slightly. "Ha ha. How odd of you to announce your return a second time. Or did you forget the events of last night? I should've remembered...a night of drinking turns you into a blank slate the next morning. Well, Fia, you had your fair share of difficulties, but I'm glad you're back safely."

Surprised, I blinked a few times. So...did I not need to report what I did in the Fourth Monster Tamer Knight Brigade? I guess I'd already made my report to him yesterday at the meat festival.

Tracing back my memory of last night, I vaguely recalled being with Cyril, Zackary, Desmond, Quentin, and Gideon...and that was it. Everything else was hazy. Even so, I must've disregarded the fact that a banquet is a nonofficial setting and reported everything to him then. An exemplary decision, if I say so myself: a model knight is never *truly* off-duty.

Seeing my grin, Cyril sighed. "Fia, it was Zackary and Quentin who reported your activities to me. All you did last night was wolf down meat and drink."

"H-huh? O-oh! You don't say." How disappointing...

"What a relief," he said with a chuckle. "You haven't changed a bit." His tone turned a little sad then. "Zackary and Quentin kept insisting you were somebody of immense importance. I was beginning to worry you'd stop making time for someone as insignificant as me."

"M-me? Important? No! No, no, you must be misunderstanding! I haven't done a single thing of note! I... *Oooh*, I get it. This must be that sarcasm thing Captain Zackary told me about! So you're actually reprimanding me for doing poorly...?" There, that made more sense.

Cyril stared at me blankly.

Agh. Elaborate, Fia! "Um...I figured that, since I failed to figure out the health of the Monster Brigade's familiars like you ordered me to and I was completely useless during the black dragon search expedition, you might be criticizing my competency...or...something?" My voice petered out to a whisper.

Cyril blinked.

Wait a second. *Now* it made sense! "D-did Captain Quentin complain about me?" Quentin was absolutely captivated by Zavilia, so I could see him getting incensed at how Zavilia did all the work while I stood loafing around. "O-or was Zackary the one who complained?"

During the fight with the Dream Bird, I'd just stood by the saints, again, loafing around. After that, I'd brushed off the majority of Zackary's questions and even collapsed into his arms, forcing him to care for me. Man...now that I thought about it, I'd really been nothing but trouble for both captains. I even cried on Zackary's uniform...

Oh no. The more I thought about it, the more I realized what a burden I'd been. I'd have to redeem myself and try harder with Quentin and Zackary next time...

"W-well," I stammered, "it's a fact that I couldn't carry out my orders, so I have no choice but to accept whatever complaints they have for me..." I trailed off again.

"You really haven't changed," said Cyril, laughing. "Yes, you haven't changed one bit. All that's different is that we've realized your true power."

"Huh?"

"It's nothing. Listen...don't worry about your inability to finish gauging the health of the familiars. The fault lies with me for recalling you early, and I doubt any would dare reprimand me—I am the captain of the top brigade, after all."

"Huh? J-just like that?" Despite spending a good few days with the Fourth Monster Tamer Knight Brigade, I'd failed to even start the one task I was assigned, and here Cyril was disregarding that with a smile.

"Don't worry about that expedition to find the black dragon either. There appears to be some discrepancy between your version of the events and that of the two captains, but they both agree that you did well. And when another captain commends one of my knights, that reflects well on me. You've done good work, Fia."

"O-okay...?" Cyril seemed earnest, but I still had my doubts. *Captain Zackary and Captain Quentin commended me? No way. Not a single thing I did yesterday could have earned me praise. I mean, Zackary did thank me for using my secret powers to help everyone, but then Quentin convinced him that it was all Zavilia's powers, not mine. If anything, Captain Zackary probably regrets thanking me at all. Why would the two commend me?*

In the end, I just couldn't bring myself to ruin the smile on Cyril's face. I decided to go with it. "I am honored to receive praise. It must be because of that, uh...one thing I did... Yep. That one thing! Did a great job with that one! The, y'know. The thing."

"Fia, you..." He paused. Rubbed his chin thoughtfully. "It's this sort of behavior that makes people expect so little of you... Although I suppose I wouldn't get through to you even if I spelled it out."

Cyril let out a defeated sigh before changing to a more cheerful tone. "How are you feeling? You wolfed down all that meat and drink last night, but you still seemed rather melancholy."

"Huh? Um, did I?" Like everything last night, it was hazy.

"Yes. You said that a dear friend of yours went somewhere far away?"

"Oooh..." Yeah, that sounded like something I'd say. Even just this morning, I was saddened by the missing warmth I used to have sleeping on my belly.

Zavilia left on a journey to become the Dragon King. He'd fought those blue dragons, so I knew he was strong, but it still sounded like a really difficult mission. He might've grown since we first met, but what if he met the same monster that caused the injuries he'd gotten when I found him?

I didn't want to be apart from him any longer. Every passing moment, my worry for him grew...

Cyril noticed my change in mood. "But it's thanks to that conversation that we became friends yesterday," he said softly.

"Uh. What?" I looked back at him blankly. Had he just said what I thought he said?

"You said that you were sad to part with your friend, so I offered to be your friend in their place. You accepted."

"N-no way!" I blurted. The alcohol might've wiped my memory, but I knew myself well enough to know I would never in a million years agree to be friends with Cyril.

I looked Cyril over, double-checking whether he was friend material for someone like me. His white knight uniform fit and flattered his slender, well-proportioned body. The tassels on his epaulets glistened, which, when combined with his handsome face, gave him an air of elegance. But that same elegant knight was also the de facto strongest swordsman in the brigade, the "Dragon of Náv." He was a cunning strategist that lived up to his position as First Knight Brigade captain, and he was also *utterly terrifying*.

I learned to fear him after the night of the first meat festival—the one after we defeated the Flower-Horned Deer. The way he cornered us using insincere praise while maintaining a false smile on his face sent shivers down my spine. And what about the time he smashed a low table in Quentin's office, all while wearing that same smile on his face to threaten Gideon? His words had been scary enough, but the way he crushed that hard low table like it was papier-mâché? The way that, even then, he'd picked up Gideon—already a teeth-chattering mess at that point—by the collar and pulled him close to threaten him some more? Only a devil could be so cruel.

On top of that, he was nobility—or I thought he must be, anyway, given the way he conducted himself. If I was right, he'd probably be high-ranking nobility to boot. High-ranking nobles were *always* a pain in the butt.

In short, he was an elite within the brigade (and thus somebody to be avoided if I didn't want to get dragged into trouble), utterly terrifying, and a high-ranking noble. No way would I agree to be his friend, not in a million-bajillion years!

"That's impossible!" I yelled. "There's *absolutely* no way I'd *ever* agree to be your friend!"

"Oh? But I thought you didn't remember what happened last night?"

Dang...I couldn't disprove what he said, but his thin smile seemed suspicious. He had to be lying, right?

"I believe trying to deny a sworn vow of friendship goes against the 'honesty' part of the Ten Knight Commandments," said Cyril, shaking his head. "Fia...honorable knights do not forget their promises."

"Urk..." I was definitely, *definitely* in the right here...but I had no way to refute him, what with my shenanigans last night. And he *knew* that I knew, which is why he wore that suspicious smile of his.

"Oh, Fia...it hurts to have you refuse me so vehemently. Why don't we just be friends? I'm an honest man, I'm adequately skilled with a sword, and I would never dream of betraying my allies. You've got a friend in me, and you'd be hard-pressed to find a better one."

Oh, heck. What a nice, pleasant smile. A smile that just screamed, 'What's the worst that could happen?'

"F-f-fine. You're no replacement for Zavilia, but...you can be my friend."

My answer seemed to amuse him. "I see your opinion remains the same, drunk or sober. Last night, you firmly insisted nobody could replace your friend, that his spot was his alone."

Wait a minute, so I'd refused him after all? But before I could say that, Cyril cut in—"Of course, you promised to open up a new spot for me right after saying that."

Drat! Normally, I'd never agree to becoming Cyril's friend. But I must've been so vulnerable after parting with Zavilia that

I'd actually agreed... Or had he just tricked me into agreeing with his silver tongue?

"Thank you, Fia," said Cyril. "I swear I'll be a good friend to you."

Either way, no fighting it now. "Th-thank you very much, uh...buddy. I'll try my best to be a good friend too." I shook his extended right hand with my own, earning a smile from him.

Presented with such a lovely, benevolent smile, I wondered if being his friend might actually turn out right. He could be kind at times, he looked after others well, and he *was* reliable—top-tier friend attributes, those. But he was such a big shot. Was I really a good match for that?

Whatever I thought, we were friends now. I began to let myself relax...and then he struck!

"Now," said Cyril, "I *do* have a request. You know, as a friend."

My eyes shot up to look him straight in the face. I'd activated his trap card... "C-Captain?! Was this the plan all along?!" *Too late to back out now...*

Still smiling, he ignored my accusation. "You said it last night, Fia: friends should talk openly with one another, spend time together, and I recall you said something about sleeping together?"

Wait, wait, wait! What's up with that last one?!

"C-Captain?! I'm okay with being your friend, but I don't sleep with friends of the opposite gender!"

"Thank goodness. I thought there was something strange when I heard you talk about a friend sleeping on your belly, of all things. I'm glad we could clear that up."

"Ngh..." *Shoot! He's framing it like it was something I said. That's not fair. I don't remember what happened!* "W-well, All right. I'm your friend now, so I guess I'll hear you out." *Time for the good ol' special move of this secret saint...changing the subject!*

"Thank you. Well, there's a place I visit every year that has a lot of memories, and I travel there so I don't forget the past. I was hoping that you could join me this time."

"Th-that sounds pretty personal, doesn't it? I'm not sure if I should come along, but I will if you insist. Where is it?"

"It falls within my domain."

A domain? Yep, this guy's a noble for sure. "By the way," I said, as casually as I could manage, "what's your family name again?"

"You make it sound like you forgot, but I'm rather sure you never knew. It's Sutherland."

"Sutherland?!" *Whoa, weird! That was the territory of my personal knight in my previous life, the Blue Knight.* "C-Captain Cyril, you're a descendant of the Blue Knight?"

Oddly enough, Cyril seemed just as surprised by my question. "You've heard of the Blue Knight? I'm surprised to hear it. The Blue Knight is rather obscure."

"Obscure? Don't the white and blue of Náv's flag come from the two strongest knights in history? How could the Blue Knight—and the White Knight, for that matter—be so obscure?"

Cyril gave me an odd look. "A white-and-blue flag, you say? Fia...that flag hasn't been flown for over three hundred years. Our flag is all red, overlaid by the coat of arms of the black dragon."

Oh...oops. The flag change was one of the first things that surprised me when I regained the memories of my past life. Náv was still the royal family, so the dynasty was the same. But if the dynasty hadn't changed, what had happened to the flag?

"Um...so the most famous knight is some Red Knight, then?"

"Red? Fia...red is a forbidden color. Nobody would dare to do such a thing."

"*Whuh?* O-oh, really?"

"Yes. Red is the color of the Great Saint. We've only once borrowed the Red of the Great Saint and have since returned it to her."

The Red of the Great Saint? I blinked, confused I'd never heard of such a thing. The hair of the Great Saint, my previous incarnation, was the exact same red as my hair now. Was there some significance there? Or were there Great Saints after my time who were also associated with red in some way?

I could tilt my head and wonder all I wanted, but I was missing three hundred years of time. No way could I come to a solid answer yet. Asking Cyril was out of the question too. He was clever enough that he might discover my big secret with a clue like that.

Time for another topic change. "I-I see. Now that you mention it, I don't ever see any red clothes or curtains or whatnot being sold. So the color was banned? That makes sense. You know what else is a good color? Blue! Like your ancestor, maybe. He was your ancestor, right?" I wasn't pretending about that; I really was interested.

Cyril smiled self-deprecatingly. "Are you really that interested? Unfortunately, no, I am not a descendant of the Blue Knight. The Blue Knight you speak of never sired any children and thus had no one to inherit the family name. When he passed away, the Sutherland territory was taken by the royal family. They managed it until thirty years ago, when it was bestowed upon my father."

"I-I see…" It felt strange to hear the fate of someone I'd spent so much time with in my past life. I wanted to ask if the Blue Knight lived a long life in good health after my passing, but that would probably be pushing my luck. Instead, I prayed that my death didn't hurt him too much…even if I was about three hundred years too late to help with that.

"Very well, Captain. Please allow me to join you. When will you be leaving?" I wanted to see that familiar blue sky and ocean as soon as possible. The Blue Knight loved Sutherland, so his grave was likely there. If I was going to Sutherland, I should visit it.

"I'm sure you'd like to rest a bit more. Let's leave in three days," he said with a smile. I agreed and left his office.

I'd been so worried that he'd request something outrageous from me, but this seemed rather mundane. I guess Cyril was a sensible man after all…

After leaving Cyril's office and walking down the hall a bit, someone called my name from behind. "Fia?" I turned around, and there stood a silver-haired, princely looking man—Fabian.

"Oh, Fabian. Is it just me, or have you gotten even princelier since we last met? What's the secret to becoming so dazzling?" I wasn't just talking about his silver hair. It was like I could see light sparkling around where he stood.

Fabian walked over to me, smiling. "Same Fia as always, saying things that us ordinary people can't hope to understand. I like that about you. How was the Fourth Monster Tamer Knight Brigade?"

I found myself stumped for an answer. "Um, between you and me, my assignment ended in failure."

"Oh?"

"Let's see...basically, Vice-Captain Gideon was in charge of the Fourth Monster Knight Tamer during Captain Quentin's long absence, but Gideon didn't like me and gave me a different assignment. So, I never ended up getting Captain Cyril's requests done."

"That's too bad. I hear they're a bit prejudiced toward other brigades, so they probably got offended that the First Knight Brigade sent someone to 'do their work for them.' Don't feel bad, everyone knows you always try your best. It's definitely not your fault," he reassured me with a smile.

What a gentleman! From his looks to his personality, he was a hundred percent princely. "Thank you, Fabian. Captain Cyril said it wasn't my fault either, but I'm worried he was just being nice."

"Ha ha! I wouldn't worry about that, Fia. Captain Cyril isn't the sort to overlook something out of kindness. Maybe for some other reason, but certainly not kindness."

"Not kindness? Then...he just expected it? Like, he thinks I'm so unreliable, I can't do anything by myself?" It made sense. To a veteran like Cyril, I was but a little child.

Fabian laughed. "You come up with the funniest of things. I have no way of knowing what's going on with the Fourth Monster Tamer Knight Brigade, but anyone with brains in their head who attended last night's banquet could see you did something big. Not just Captain Cyril and Captain Desmond, but even Captain Zackary, Captain Quentin, and Vice-Captain Gideon were glued to your side."

"Huh? Um..."

"Oh, no, you don't have to tell me anything. Whatever you did, a gag order was issued to keep the lid on it... Although, there's something odd about it. The gag order doesn't apply to you." He paused for a moment and muttered to himself, as if wondering aloud. "You're free to say what you want, it seems."

I blinked a few times, surprised at Fabian's insight. First the captains and now Fabian? Why was everyone around me so capable? It was going to start getting me jealous.

I frowned at Fabian, but he just continued on obliviously. "By the way, I heard Captain Cyril is to visit the Duchy of Sutherland as the representative of His Highness the Crown Prince Saviz."

"...Huh?" *Did he say Sutherland?! As in, the Sutherland that Captain Cyril and I are visiting? Captain Cyril made it sound like we were going on some excursion together for private business, but is it an official work trip? As the freakin' representative of the crown prince?!*

"F-Fabian, you don't by any chance mean as the commander's representative, do you? Instead of the, uh, crown prince?!" If he did mean the Crown Prince, that would make the visit some kind of super-important state-level business!

Fabian didn't catch how flustered I was. He sounded downright casual, in fact. "No, I meant the crown prince. There was a conflict in the duchy a while ago—they call it the 'Lament of Sutherland.' Since then, the royal family has visited every year to show respect for those who died."

"N-nobody said the visit was official state business! If he's using a representative, is Commander Saviz too busy to go himself? B-but why would the Commander—I mean, His Highness the Crown Prince—choose Captain Cyril to go? I guess being captain of the First Knight Brigade means he carries out this stuff, huh?"

"No, Captain Cyril isn't going as captain but as the Duke of Sutherland, with a right to the th—"

"Fia." A voice called my name, interrupting Fabian.

I turned around, and there he was...Saviz himself! It was already weird running into all these acquaintances this morning, but now I'd up and bumped into the SS-rank super high-profile Commander himself!

Fabian and I turned to face Saviz and performed the knight salute. Saviz approached with broad steps and looked down at me. "I heard you're going to Sutherland with Cyril, yes? There's... something we must discuss. Come to my place later with Cyril."

I had a feeling he wasn't having us over to wish us a good journey.

Captain Cyril, you're tricky as ever. Making this out to be some casual visit...!

After Saviz left, Fabian and I went to training. It'd been a while since I last trained, but I couldn't focus. I was too concerned about my upcoming meeting with Saviz. What did he want to talk to *me* for? Still, the poetry teacher praised me—

"Well done. You've *finally* eked out a sensible poem."

Fabian agreed. "Your poems are a lot better when you're only half focused."

Honestly, I wasn't sure how I felt about that.

During chess practice, another familiar face appeared... Desmond. Today was just full of chance encounters.

He didn't seem as chatty as usual, and he occasionally stole glances up at me as we played. Before long, he was mumbling something indistinct under his breath before finally steeling himself and looking me in the eye. "So, Fia... I hear you have a familiar."

"Yes, I do..." I began, then remembered all the time I'd spent practicing the fine art of stretching the truth. A while back, Cyril suggested I exaggerate my familiar's ability so I wouldn't be looked down on by the Fourth Monster Tamer Knight Brigade, where hierarchy was largely determined by the strength of one's familiar. Unfortunately, when I tried to do so to Gideon, it had an opposite effect and caused him to believe Zavilia was actually the weakest monster there was.

I didn't want to repeat that failure, so I'd practiced and practiced, pretending I was speaking to Saviz and Cyril. I glanced up at Desmond. It was time to put what I practiced to the test.

"I do," I said, "but my familiar is...how do you put it? Special. Unparalleled, even. It's a sort of blackish, dragonish, kingish type of beast...maybe you've heard of it?"

Since Zavilia was already a black dragon, I had to exaggerate by making Desmond think Zavilia was something even greater—like what he was aiming to become, a Black Dragon King. Not that I really knew the difference.

"F-Fia, stop! Not another word further!" Desmond barked. "I wasn't asking what your familiar was! Please, just hold your tongue! You're putting me in danger here!"

"Wha-huh?"

"I already know, all right?! I know your familiar is the strongest, wickedest monster there is! So please, not another word!" he shrieked, holding his hands out defensively. He sounded genuinely terrified of my familiar.

Whoa.

I guess my special practice paid off!

I stood and slammed both hands onto the chess table, trembling with excitement. "I-I did it! My training worked!"

Desmond trembled too, for different reasons. "W-well, I'd better get going. But let me make one thing clear though, Fia: I didn't pressure you into exposing your familiar's identity. Not one bit. Right?" He looked up at the ceiling as he spoke.

Weird as he was being, I saw no reason to disagree. "Right."

He let out a heavy sigh of relief and, still facing the ceiling, spoke. "Did you hear that?! I didn't coerce her or anything!"

What was up with this guy? Had Weirdo Quentin Syndrome spread to Desmond? Was there some kind of contagion that infected only knight captains? This could be a major problem. But then again, they weren't my captains, and I didn't have the clout to change anything even if there was something strange going on. Ultimately, I decided it was best to pretend I didn't see anything.

Then again, who was a rank-and-file knight like me to tell a captain what kind of behavior was right and wrong, anyway?

Evening neared, and so I went to the office of Saviz with Cyril. His office was actually a separate building known as the House of the Black Shield, situated so that it was enclosed on all sides by the brigade buildings. The First Knight Brigade building was right next to the House of the Black Shield, so I'd often wondered just what was inside its lavish exterior.

Full of excitement, I stepped through the entrance...and leaped back in shock at what I saw above me.

Cyril offered an understanding smile. "Oh, this must be your first time seeing this portrait. This is Her Holiness, the legendary Great Saint."

I already knew *that*. I knew the Great Saint's face like it was my own, because...well, it *had* been!

Just past the entrance of the House of the Black Shield was a spacious atrium, three-stories high. The sudden vastness of the space was breathtaking, but not as breathtaking as the enormous portrait displayed in the back of the atrium for all to see. It depicted a young woman clad in a black dress. Her knee-length red hair swayed in the wind. A single scarlet rose was wrapped around her wrist.

Oooh... That's my combat outfit! I'd always made sure to wear a black dress and a rose around my wrist when I went to battle. The portrait was accurate, but...I looked so awfully prim and proper. It was incredibly embarrassing. Unconsciously, I took a step back, then a second—and felt my back hit the entrance door.

Cyril looked at me curiously. "Is something the matter, Fia? Are you feeling overwhelmed by the portrait of the Great Saint?"

"Um, no, I, uh, I was just thinking that since this is the personal building of Saviz, the commander of the knight brigades..." Flustered, I spouted off the first excuse that came to mind. "It'd make more sense to have a portrait of some renowned knight instead of the Great Saint, y-you know?"

"Oh, I see," Cyril said, turning to look up at the portrait. "I understand why you might think that, but this portrait has been here for three hundred years."

"F-for three hundred years? I-I see. Hah...wow, can't believe nobody's had time to change the portrait out since then, right?"

Sure, I did seal away the Demon Lord in my past life, but I'd died young. The actual time I was even active as the Great Saint was pretty brief, so you'd think they'd display a portrait of some other Great Saint who had lived longer and achieved more.

As though reading my mind, Cyril continued. "It's not so much that there haven't been opportunities to change the portrait. We simply *cannot* change it. The first commander of the Náv Black Dragon Knights ordered this portrait to hang here forevermore."

"He did *what*?" The Náv Black Dragon Knights didn't exist at the time of my previous life, so I wasn't acquainted with the first commander at all. Why would they be so insistent that a portrait of me remain up?

"Could it be?" I muttered to myself. "Did I have a fan?"

People loved to make the past sound more glorious than it was. A skilled minstrel could weave the story of a young girl giving her life to seal away the Demon Lord into a grand legend.

"Then again," I mused, "history *has* already been rewritten a bit." In recorded history, the Great Saint had apparently married the hero who sealed away the Demon Lord with her, and their descendants later formed the royal family. But the Náv Royal Family had existed long before my previous lifetime, and the line continued, uninterrupted.

So why make up that story? Had there been some demand for a "reformed" royal family? Creating a new flag and the knight brigades would certainly help with something like that...

"Hmmmmm..." I was completely stumped.

"Are you all right, Fia?" asked Cyril worriedly. "You've been talking to yourself for a while now."

"Huh?" I hurriedly pulled myself together and smiled. "Ah, f-forgive me. I'm okay."

"If you're feeling ill or something, please let me know." Cyril still sounded a bit worried, but we headed for Saviz's office anyhow.

Saviz's office was imposing. That's what struck me first. The room was abnormally spacious, enough to fit multiple captain's offices in, and those were already spacious enough. At the back of the office was a desk, and the wall behind it was lined with elegant sculptures. The sides of the desk were draped with the flag of the Náv Black Dragon Knights, and the side walls displayed tons of swords and shields.

Yeah, this is definitely the office of a military man, all right.

Saviz appeared to be doing paperwork, but around him were a dozen or so knights on standby. A few of the knights were familiar faces from the First Knight Brigade, likely on guard duty.

A knight waiting at the entrance led us to the sofa. Once there, Cyril and I waited for permission to be seated.

Saviz quickly stood up from the desk and walked over to us. "You may sit," he said. Only after he had sat down himself, however, did we sit. He looked at me silently for a few seconds before opening his mouth to speak. "I heard you will be departing to Sutherland with Cyril in three days."

"Yes, sir," I answered. Not that I knew why exactly I was going, or for what. All I knew was that it wasn't going to be the leisurely visit Cyril had made it out to be.

Oblivious to my internal grumblings, Cyril spoke up. "I haven't explained anything to Fia yet. I reckoned it would be best to wait until you were present, Commander."

"I see," said Saviz curtly, putting a finger to his lips in thought. "All right, then. Fia, ten years ago, there was a conflict in Sutherland. For many of the people there, the scars of that conflict haven't faded. As the ones deemed responsible for that conflict, we—the knight brigade—cannot expect a warm welcome."

He traced his long finger over the eyepatch on his right eye.

"You're still in training, so I do not want you to go there as a knight," he said. "You will visit as someone who will one day become a knight. Look at Sutherland objectively. Decide for yourself who was at fault with your own eyes." He spoke quietly, his lone eye brimming with complex emotion.

His explanation was too cryptic for me to discern his true intent, but I knew this was a request I couldn't possibly refuse... not that refusal was ever on the table. When the Commander told you to jump, you could either say, "Yes, sir!" or "How high?"

"Understood," I said. "I will travel to Sutherland with Captain Cyril."

Cyril relaxed at that, slumping his shoulders. "Fia, the Sutherlanders are fervent worshippers of the Great Saint. I wished I myself had known that ten years ago."

"The Great Saint? Not saints in general?" I asked. Just how many Great Saints were there, anyway? And why go out of the way to worship one instead of all saints? "Er, how many Great Saints have there been again? And do you know which one's the most popular? The top five, maybe?"

Agh, I'd gone and blurted that out without thinking. Did I even want to know the answer? What if I was a nobody after all those hundreds of years? It had been a while. Maybe I'd better expect the worst...

"Naturally, Her Holiness Serafina would be the most popular."

"Really?!" *S-Serafina?! That was me! I-I'm number one?!* I put my hands on my cheeks and grinned.

Cyril nodded. "Of course, that's not terribly surprising. There's only ever *been* one Great Saint."

"Huh...? *Really?!*" Just one Great Saint?! "O-oh! Lucky her, winning first place by default!" And here I was thinking I was popular instead of just the only option. I hung my head dejectedly.

"Cyril is right, Fia," said Saviz. "The people of Sutherland are devout believers in the Great Saint."

"Right. That's what we were talking about." I looked up at Saviz, meeting his fierce eyes.

"There's no telling how they might react to you, with your hair and eye color matching the legendary Great Saint's. Don't be alone, not even for a single moment."

"Oh. Oooh! Right. I'll be careful." Made sense. My hair and eyes were the *exact same color* as in my previous life. That being the case...

"Such a combination of colors is incredibly rare," said Saviz. "Make sure you're careful."

"Yes, sir." ...I'd rather refuse going to Sutherland altogether. But it was Saviz we were talking about. Refusal wasn't an option.

The Commander said the combination of my hair and eye colors were rare, but is it really? I thought to myself as I walked back to the dorm. *I can't refute him, but surely these colors were common...enough...?*

Now that I thought about it, people had often told me in my past life that they'd never seen anyone else with such red hair.

"Your hair is as scarlet as blood. Just how beloved by the spirits are you?"

"With hair that color, you must have saint's blood! Your potential must be limitless!"

People went on and on like that. Looking back, I wondered if I really *had* ever seen anyone else with hair as close to the color of blood. Perhaps it actually was pretty rare?

Forgive me, Commander, I get it now. You were completely right.

It was the first time in a while that I'd thought back to my past life so much. Maybe that's why, after turning in early for the night, I dreamt of my past life for the first time.

In my dream, Canopus—my personal knight, the famed Blue Knight himself—looked down at me. His waist-length dark-blue hair swayed, and his shapely face was locked in a frown. "Your Highness, how many times must I explain it before you learn?!"

Ho ho ho! Oh, silly Canopus, thought the dream-me. *You know I'll never learn no matter how many times you tell me.*

Not that I'd say that out loud. "Forgive me for being unable to learn, Canopus," I said, slyly trying to look meek. "I must cause you so much grief."

"Your Highness! Please…" He shook his head. "Spare me the act! Jeez…how can the peerless Great Saint be such a headache?!"

Good job, Canopus. I should've known my own personal knight wouldn't be tricked by such a superficial facade.

The dream-me dropped the act and smiled. "I'm sorry for being such a handful, but I simply had to see your territory as soon as possible. That's why I was in a bit of a rush."

"A bit? A bit?!" He broke into laughter. "You call riding full tilt for two days without rest, changing horses as you go…that's 'a bit'?! In what world?"

"I'm sorry," said dream-me dejectedly. It looked like I had genuinely worried poor Canopus.

He let out a resigned sigh and then knelt before me. "I beg you, before you do anything rash again, think about my purpose. I am your personal knight. I exist to serve and protect you."

"I know. From the bottom of my heart, Canopus…I apologize for being so impulsive."

Only then did Canopus's frown finally clear. "As long as you understand." He bowed low enough for his head to touch the ground. "I am deeply humbled to have Her Holiness the Great Saint, the Second Princess Serafina Náv, pay a visit to my territory. I, and all my people, welcome you with open arms."

Behind him, some locals peered at us through a door held slightly ajar. A single glimpse of their smiles was all I needed to see how much they loved their lord.

Hey, Canopus. I'm going to check on Sutherland for you.

A Tale of the Secret Saint

26
The Visit to Sutherland Part 1

"*Oh, me, oh, my? What is this?*
La-lee-la!
Such a beautiful rock! It twinkles so bright!
Is it a chunk of a star? That fell from the night??
Tee-ta-dah!"

I tried to speak in rhyme as I held up the shiny rock I'd found. A hand reached out and grabbed it from me.

"I think this is just an ordinary rock, Fia," said Fabian, even though he'd only looked at it for a second! He handed the rock back to me. "Ha ha! Are you still practicing poetry? The more you practice, the further from poetry your writing seems to get. Maybe you should stop practicing?"

I was a little hesitant to part with my shiny rock, but—after one last look—I set it back down on the ground. I guess my bag would be filled to the brim if I took everything that caught my attention with me. Oh well.

We were currently traveling south toward Sutherland as a unit. The Kingdom of Náv was situated on a continent surrounded by ocean on every side but the east. Sutherland was located at the Kingdom's farthest southern coast, and it was about a ten-day trip by horse carriage.

Our unit was composed of eighty First Knight Brigade knights. Cyril made sure many of the younger knights, including Fabian, came along too—to learn history, he said. Twenty civil officials joined us as well. Most of them couldn't ride horses, instead traveling by horse carriage. That slowed us to a snail's pace, even though all us knights were on horseback.

"Break time is over! We'll be moving soon!"

I turned toward the source of the voice, a noble standing at the center of the knights—Cyril. He was acting as the crown prince's representative, so he looked more like a noble than a knight. That way, any passersby could see that the visit was indeed a serious, formal affair.

Cyril's noble clothes were embroidered in shiny gold and silver threads. Over them, he wore a dark-purple mantle fastened at the neck by a large jewel. His chest was adorned with countless medals, and a golden aiguillette that glistened with sunlight extended from his mantle. On anyone else, such an outfit would have looked outlandish, pretentious...but Cyril wore it well.

From a distance, I had to admit that he looked the very image of a high-ranking noble. Saviz made the right choice selecting Cyril as his representative. When heading into not-so-friendly territory, it was important to make a good impression. Cyril cleaned up nicely, so I was sure the people of Sutherland would think well of him.

I mounted my horse and rode up alongside Fabian. Everything always looks so dazzling from atop a horse. And going to new places is a joy too. Being able to see new sights, experience new foods—it was all just so wonderful.

Knights must've been uncommon this far out, as some children waved at us as we passed. I smiled and waved back, prompting them to throw a flower crown wreath at me. I caught it and wore it on my head at once, much to their delight.

As I giggled, Fabian said, "You're amazing, Fia. You always manage to find a way to enjoy yourself, no matter when it is or who you're with."

"Huh? What brought this on all of a sudden?"

"It's something I've been thinking about for a while. You have many skills, but your greatest is that you can spend time happily with anyone, anytime." He fixed his eyes on me.

"Really? Can't everyone do that?"

"You have a rosy view. But I doubt whether I or Captain Cyril, or any of the captains, or even the Commander for that matter, would fit into your *everyone*."

"Huh. Is that right?" I looked at him, hoping he'd say more, but he just met my gaze and softly laughed.

Yeah, Fabian's got this side to him too. He can play mean and withhold information when he sees that I really want to know something.

My eyes shot wide open—*tell meee!*—but he just laughed me off.

The mood was light when we set off, but conversation petered out as we neared our destination. This journey was an annual event, so it wasn't the first visit for many of the knights. Saviz had mentioned that the knight brigade were unwelcome in Sutherland... Maybe they were remembering that?

Passersby weren't waving at us anymore. Occasionally, they'd stop what they were doing and bow their heads, but there were no more smiles.

Once we moved deeper into Sutherland, it became even more apparent that we weren't welcome. The immediate lack of people leapt out at me first. Notice of our visit should've been sent ahead, so they would have known a royal representative was coming...yet no citizens could be seen. Normally, there would've been a big welcome, with people lining both sides of the road, but there was hardly a soul present. I could see a few citizens here and there in the far distance, but they all kept their heads down.

Um...what's going on? Weren't the people of Sutherland nicer than this?

I racked my brain for any information I could remember about the Sutherlanders. Most of them were descendants of people who lived on an island south of Náv. Sutherland itself was originally formed when the island's volcano erupted, and the people needed somewhere to flee to. The Sutherlanders had dark-brown skin and dark-blue hair. They were good-natured people that laughed easily and could never stay still...or so I remembered them. I'd only visited this land once in my past life, and I'd been accompanied by its lord, Canopus, then. There was no telling if they were just acting that way for their leader.

We kept moving forward, and I kept reminiscing in a half daze about my previous life's memories. All the while, it was quiet as a funeral.

Only Fabian spoke. "I had no idea Captain Cyril was treated so coldly by his own subjects. To think not a single person came out to greet their returning lord..."

Straight ahead was the lord's mansion itself, Cyril's home.

Oh... I know this place. My cheeks warmed at the sight of it. The mansion's colors, blue and white, paired well with the coastline. The building as a whole seemed to glow warmly in the sunlight. It hadn't changed at all in the past three hundred years.

I was off my horse and unpacking my things when I heard hoofbeats in the distance. My curiosity piqued, I looked toward the gate and saw a group of knights I had never seen before—the Thirteenth Knight Brigade who oversaw this area.

A man with the air of a captain dismounted the finest of the horses. He was a tall man, with hair and skin that were well baked by the sun. He had the fine muscles of someone who'd trained often, but...

How is he so weak? He was far and away the weakest of any captain I'd seen so far.

The man who seemed to be the Thirteenth Knight Brigade captain turned to Cyril and bowed deeply. "It's been a while, Captain Cyril. Thank you for coming all this way."

Cyril let out an exasperated sigh. "How many times have I told you, Kurtis? You're a captain now, you don't need to be so formal. Just call me Cyril."

"Then why do you still address me formally, Captain Cyril?"

"Because I'm used to it. I can't stop so easily."

"It's the same for me. After all the years I've worked under you, no way can I consider myself your equal." Kurtis's eyes were earnest.

Cyril sighed softly and turned Kurtis to face us. "I'm sure many of you among the First Knight Brigade have yet to meet him, so allow me to introduce Captain Kurtis of the Thirteenth Knight Brigade."

Kurtis was a tall man somewhere in his early thirties with sunbaked light-blue hair that came down to his shoulders. He smiled, revealing pure-white teeth that stood out against his tan skin.

"It's a pleasure to meet everyone from the First Knight Brigade. I am Kurtis Bannister, captain of the Thirteen Knight Brigade." His shapely face and quiet greeting made him feel more like a well-built civil official. He just didn't have the intensity I'd seen in all the other captains.

Seeing him, I realized just how well put together Cyril, Desmond, Quentin, and Zackary were as captains. They gave off this potency that made you want to follow them. Kurtis, on the other hand, seemed reserved, unassertive, and quiet. Could a captain like him really capture the hearts of the power-worshipping knights?

As I stared at him, his gaze suddenly met mine, and his eyes shot open in an instant. "The duchess!"

"Whuh?" I squeaked out, but Kurtis made no sign he noticed, remaining wide-eyed. I turned to Fabian. "Is he...talking about me? Like he thinks I have the elegance of a duchess or something?"

"I *seriously* doubt that," said Cyril, stoically. "To be honest, I'm amazed that's where your mind went. Don't you think he's simply mistaking you for the Duchess of Sutherland?"

"Huh?! So, um...does that mean there's a Duke of Sutherland too?" My loud voice seemed to draw attention. Other knights were beginning to look at me.

H-huh? Did I say something weird? They stared at me, astonished. I took a couple of nervous steps back and—oops—bumped right into Cyril. He stared down at me for a few moments before donning a beautiful—and oh-so-fake—smile.

"A pleasure, Lady Fia. I am Cyril, Duke of Sutherland," he said as he pulled his left leg back, moved his right hand to his chest, and slightly lowered his head—the gentleman's bow.

Ugh. He was obviously mocking me, but he so flawlessly carried off the high-class noble shtick that I was kind of at a loss for words.

In my silence, Cyril righted his posture and lightly shook his head. "You really don't have any interest in me, do you, Fia? The that fact I'm a duke is just as well known as the fact that I'm the

First Knight Brigade captain. Have you really never asked anyone about me?"

"U-um...w-well, I'd rather see things with my own eyes instead of learn everything through gossip."

"How admirable. Although you'd likely never learn anything about me in the first place, considering your critical lack of curiosity. The other day, I told you that the land of Sutherland was bestowed upon my father...but I omitted the fact that he received this gift by renouncing his royal status and becoming a vassal of the kingdom. My father was the younger brother of the previous king."

My eyes went wide. "You're a descendant of the previous king's little brother?!"

Whoa...I never would've imagined that Cyril had royal blood, not in a million years. But it did make sense. Sutherland was a large and fertile land. It wouldn't be given to just anyone, and a former royal was the perfect recipient. It also made sense now, why Cyril was standing in for Saviz. Who better to represent royalty than someone with royal lineage?

"I-I knew you had to be a high-ranking noble for someone to bestow this land on you, but I had no idea you were a duke," I said.

He raised his hands defeatedly. "I'm just amazed that something everyone knows could surprise you. If you have any other questions, please ask them now. I fear you might have some grand misunderstanding if your doubts are left as is."

I gulped, then asked the question that had been lingering in my mind since Kurtis called out to me. "Um...was I mistaken for a duchess because I look like your wife?"

Completely silent, Cyril opened his eyes just a smidge. Had I said something silly? I spun my own words around my head a few times...and then it hit me. Oh no.

"W-w-wait! I-I wasn't asking because I'm into you or anything, okay?!"

Cyril let out a great, forced-sounding sigh. "Let's address that, Fia. I continue to be shocked at just how little you know about me."

"Huh? Um...?"

"I am a bachelor. Full name: Cyril Sutherland. Twenty-seven years old. 187 centimeters. Parents have passed on. No siblings. Second in line for the throne. Duke and captain of the First Knight Brigade."

"S-second in line for the throne?!"

"You didn't know that either? Just what *do* you know about me?"

"U-um, I know you're a knight with gray hair and blue eyes!"

"Anybody who sees me could see that. Then again, I suppose I'm the fool for expecting anything more from you." He heaved another sigh before continuing in a weary voice. "The duchess to whom Kurtis was referring is my mother. She passed away ten years ago and had red hair like yours. Many of the people living here are former islanders with dark blue hair. Red hair, while common enough in the Kingdom, is *incredibly* rare here. That's probably why he mistook you for my mother. Ha! A world with you as my mother...now *that's* a nightmarish thought."

I ignored Cyril's last aside and turned to Kurtis. "C-Captain Kurtis, I'm only fifteen years old! Do you really think I could have such a big child? Even if it were possible..." I gestured at Cyril and let out a *hmph*! "I refuse! I refuse to have such a talented but stubborn child as him!"

"Ah, f-forgive me." Kurtis rushed over and clasped my hand. "My eyesight is a little weak. All I could make out at a distance was your red hair, something I haven't seen in Sutherland for ten years. Ah, yes—looking closely now, I can see you're a beautiful, dignified knight. I must've mistaken that air of dignity for the noble air of the duchess."

"Heh...heh heh heh...you don't say!" I turned to Fabian and beamed impishly. "You hear that, Fabian? I had the elegance of a duchess after all!"

"You're really taking all of *that* at face value? You really do always find a way to enjoy yourself." He shrugged, exasperated.

H-huh? He did say that before, but...why do I feel like he means something different now...? F-Fabian! What's wrong with enjoying a compliment now and then?!

Hmm...did I bring too little? I couldn't help but wonder that after I entered the room I'd been assigned and put down my stuff.

We were to stay in Sutherland for ten days, lodging at Cyril's mansion all the while. As I unpacked my luggage, I couldn't help but think about how incredible it was that Cyril's mansion had enough rooms for all one hundred of us, even if there had to sometimes be a few per room.

After we settled in, we gathered and went over the planned schedule. For the time being, we were to peacefully spend our time making contact with the locals. And then, seven days from now, we would have a ceremony offering prayers to Sutherlanders who'd lost their lives.

"Captain Cyril lost his mother, the duchess, in Sutherland ten years ago."

The room instantly fell silent. According to the explanation that followed, Cyril's father—the duke at the time—was present when she died. He blamed the Sutherlanders for her death and ordered the knights to attack the populace. The ensuing conflict lasted only two days, but the vast disparity in strength led to the deaths of several hundred Sutherlanders. It wasn't long before the full details of the incident came to light, but official charges brought against the citizens of Sutherland didn't clearly state whether they were guilty or innocent.

An unforeseeable accident caused the duchess to fall into the ocean.

"The citizens bear no fault for the incident but showed no efforts to save her, leading to her death."

Facing such facts, the Kingdom declared that *"the people of Sutherland had an opportunity to save the duchess but chose not to do so."*

This declaration angered the Sutherlanders. The people's resentment only grew when the Kingdom took pity on Cyril's family and let them retain their title and land. The family had lost both the duchess in the "unforeseeable accident" and the duke in the fighting that followed.

Ten years later, and the Sutherlanders still resented the family and the knights who had murdered their kind. To calm things down, the Kingdom accepted some responsibility and started the tradition of annual royal visits to pray for the citizens who'd died in the "Lament of Sutherland."

Hmm. There was a lot to think about. It didn't sound like the citizens were at fault if you asked me. The ocean currents moved fast and trying to save someone from them could be just as dangerous for the rescuer. No one could blame the citizens for hesitating to jump in after the duchess...and yet many of their people were slaughtered as punishment. The kingdom itself ruled that the citizens' refusal to act was unjust, but what of the knights? They were let off with nothing more than slaps on the wrist. Throw in the fact that the same duke's family that ordered the attack was allowed to carry on governing the land, and you kinda started to wonder how there hadn't been a revolt.

Objectively speaking, the citizens had no obligation to forgive anyone. They could easily find an excuse to refuse the yearly royal visits or otherwise protest, but instead they chose to accept the apology.

Yeah...the people of Sutherland are still kind after all these years.

I cleared my mind and thought back to three hundred years ago, to the Sutherlanders who had smiled so happily at me. They showed me kindness, saying they were happy to have the Great Saint here. They made me delicious food, picked beautiful flowers for me, and told me all sorts of wonderful tales. They stayed by my side at every moment, always gentle and friendly and faithful.

If possible, I wanted them and Cyril to make amends. Cyril was kind and caring too—he looked after everyone in his brigade as if they were his own children (and yes, I know now that he's unmarried!) I was certain that he'd show the people of Sutherland the same care, if given the chance. I bet that'd made the cold reception from the citizens hurt Cyril even more.

If only they knew what he was really like.

I stood up and moved to the window. Looking out, I could see the beautiful expanse of Sutherland, surrounded by ocean and mountains.

Perhaps Sutherland was a place of sadness to Cyril. A decade ago, he would've only been seventeen when he lost both parents one after the other. It would have been one thing if he'd lost them to natural causes or disease, but an unforeseeable accident and a terrible conflict would've been all too much. He was probably filled with regret, constantly wondering if he could've done something to prevent their fates. Worse yet, the citizens his parents had sworn to protect were killed because of them, erecting an insurmountable wall between him and his subjects.

Yeah...I'm sure Cyril is suffering right now.

"Hey, Fia, we're free to do whatever we want today. Why don't we take a look around together?"

I blinked, pulled out of my daze by the sudden question. Everyone had left the room some time ago, leaving only Fabian and me.

"Fabian! S-sorry," I said hurriedly. "My mind was elsewhere. Yes, let's have a look around!"

He smiled. "Thank goodness. Now I don't have to look around by myself. Is there anywhere you want to go?"

"We could go anywhere? Then how about the beach? And then the town!"

"Is this your first time in Sutherland?"

"Huh? O-oh, yeah, mm-hmm! First time ever." Of course, it wasn't really my first time—I'd come in my past life, but that visit had only lasted a few hours and I'd never even set foot outside the lord's mansion. In a sense, this really was my first time seeing Sutherland.

"I've always wanted to see Sutherland's beach," I said. "And the way the sun reflects off of the white walls of the town..." In my past life, I'd promised the Sutherlanders that I'd soak in the surroundings the next time I came by. I never did get to fulfill that promise. Maybe I could do it in this life.

We walked to the beach first. A salty sea breeze blew in. The sand crunched pleasantly under my feet. I stopped for a moment to take in my surroundings. The beautiful blue sea stretched endlessly. This was the land Canopus had loved...the land that the people undoubtedly loved too, three hundred years later.

A wave struck the shore, and a gust of wind whipped across my face. "Eee! My hair's gonna get all messed up!" I hurried to hold my hair down.

At that moment, a cute voice shouted out at me from behind. "It's the Great Saint!"

I turned around. A few young children around the age of five or six stood there, staring up at me, their eyes brimming with admiration. "Red hair! Golden eyes! It's the Great Saint!"

One after another, they ran up and latched on to me. I tried to crouch down and brace myself but fell over on my behind by the time the third child got me.

"Aha ha ha ha! It's the Great Saint!"

The children laughed as more of them latched on to me, and I soon found myself laughing too. "Aha ha ha ha! You're all so strong! You knocked me down!"

I rolled over to escape and began tickling the children, laughing all the while.

"You look like you're having fun, Fia," said a voice from above. The children and I turned around to see Cyril and Kurtis standing there.

"O-oh, Captain Cyril! I'm just, uh, doing some training." I quickly got to my feet and faced the two, taking a moment to glance at the children. Their faces were clouded now.

H-huh? But they were laughing so much only seconds ago. I glanced back and forth between the children and the captains. It wasn't like the captains had sprouted fangs or horns or whatever—they weren't monsters. Why were the kids so scared? As I thought that, one of the children suddenly bolted away. Like a chain reaction, one kid after another began to run. Soon enough, not a single one was in sight.

I smiled, watching the kids fly away like a gust of wind. "Heh! They're an energetic bunch, aren't they?"

Cyril squinted slightly. "Indeed. It'd be nice if they could live healthy and happy lives."

"Well, I'm sure they will under your rule!" I said confidently.

"I wonder," he said with a troubled smile. "They *did* just run off at the sight of me, after all."

O-oh...right. The people here didn't think kindly of knights and the Sutherland family. The children probably couldn't tell that it was Cyril because he was in his knight uniform...but they still ran. In fact, the uniforms might've been what set them running in the first place.

I looked up at Cyril and Kurtis. They were a lot taller than the average person. Maybe that scared those short kids?

"Um..." Now I was desperate to change the topic. "Are you two close?" I asked the captains.

Kurtis smiled softly, perhaps reading my intent. "I used to be a knight of the First Knight Brigade, meaning I worked under Captain Cyril. It'd be a bit impudent of me to say that we're close."

"Really?! You were in the First Knight Brigade?! You're an elite too, then!"

Kurtis laughed. "You're a knight of the First Knight Brigade, right? Wouldn't that make you an elite as well?"

I blinked. "Huh?"

Cyril cut in. "Kurtis, I'm not so sure whether to call Fia an elite. Let's leave it at that for now."

"You're not? But you can read people better than anyone! You're saying there's someone that even you can't put a finger on?!" Kurtis exclaimed, looking me over.

"Oh, I see. She has the same red hair and golden eyes as the Great Saint," Kurtis muttered to himself. "I could see why you'd have some difficulties judging her..." He shook the thought off and turned back to me. "Three years ago, it was Captain Cyril who recommended me—an ordinary knight at the time—for the position of Thirteenth Knight Brigade captain. I didn't have the achievements nor the ability to be captain back then and, as such, I was met with reasonable opposition...but Captain Cyril supported me regardless," he said, a nostalgic gleam in his eye.

"You were a part of my brigade for five years," said Cyril. "And every one of those years, you accompanied me on my visit to Sutherland. The people here bear a grudge against us and avoid us at every turn, but you somehow found a way to be accepted by them. Your predecessor, the former Thirteenth Knight Brigade captain, could never have done such a thing. That's why I recommended you for the captain position in the first place."

"Ha ha...I appreciate the thought, but I'm terribly weak compared to the other captains. Guess I should thank my lucky stars for my rapport with the locals, eh?" Kurtis joked.

Cyril glared. "None of that, Kurtis. You *are* strong enough. You wouldn't be a captain if you weren't."

"Thank you for your concern, but it's unnecessary. I'm past the point of comparing myself to other captains. I know that all I need to worry about is my own strengths and how to best use them."

Cyril sighed softly. "Kurtis, forgive me, I should know better than to doubt you." All of a sudden, he seemed a little nervous... and then he looked at me.

I met his eyes. *Is he going to ask me something?* He frowned for a moment, before seemingly making up his mind about something and dropping to one knee to match my height.

"C-Captain?!"

He suddenly grabbed my hand. "Fia, there's something I'd like to request of you. I'm asking as your friend, so you do have the right to refuse."

"O-okay?" *Another request? Seriously?!*

"The people of this land are fervent worshippers of the Great Saint and, as such, place significance in red hair. Those children called you the Great Saint because red hair is synonymous with her legend here. However..." He paused for a moment and looked at my red hair. "By now, you've surely heard about the Lament of Sutherland from ten years ago, yes? That incident all began with my mother..."

Cyril paused for a moment. "My...*red-haired* mother. She was never accepted by the Sutherlanders, and her looks were striking enough that those of a certain age will associate you with her. At the same time, your hair is the same color as the Great Saint's, so they'll surely have conflicting feelings about that. What I'm trying to say is this: The past is fresh in the minds of Sutherland's people. For better or worse, your hair will stir up the citizens."

I stared back at him blankly. *This...just got really complicated.*

"Time stopped for the people of Sutherland on that fateful day ten years ago," said Cyril. "It will take a shock to the system for Sutherland to move on. I think you and your red hair can be that shock."

"A shock?"

"You probably don't remember, but you once lectured me about the way saints should truly be. Your words that night resonated deeply with me. If I merely wanted to free the Sutherlanders from their past, I could've brought any red-haired woman along. But if I'm to change Sutherland for the better, I need someone with a strong will. I need you to be the one to change them."

"With...my *hair*?" I could barely believe what I was hearing.

"Granted, the past is still deeply rooted among the people. You alone won't be enough to fix such a deep rift, so please don't feel guilty if we don't make progress by the time we leave. Still... even with just ten days, I believe you're exactly the person who can get the job done."

"Um, I-I...?" *This whole trip felt so much more serious all of a sudden... What do I do?!*

"Of course, you still have the right to refuse. The citizens have strong feelings about red hair. They may resent you for it. You may even find yourself in danger because of it. If you choose to refuse, I can have you work inside the mansion for the duration of our stay. And allow me to apologize for not telling you sooner. I wanted you to see Sutherland and to form your own opinion of this place first before asking such a thing of you."

I silently stared at Cyril, unable to think of a response. Even for such an important thing, he didn't force or pressure me into anything. His expression was so placid. Looking closely, however, I could see that his blue eyes were clouded and dark.

He was suffering.

I could tell from his words that he genuinely wanted to help the citizens. He'd probably tried countless things over the ten years that he was lord, only to meet with failure each time. I was his last chance.

Our relationship was one of captain and subordinate. He could've easily ordered me to do what he wanted and been done with it. But instead, he'd gone out of his way to forge a friendship with me, just to give me a right to refuse. He was remarkably kindhearted.

It wasn't right that the people of Sutherland couldn't feel that kindness, and it wasn't right that the equally kind people of Sutherland had to live with such resentment in their hearts.

I thought back to the almost completely deserted streets I'd seen. The few people who showed up kept their distance, making no effort to show us any welcome. The difference between their blank faces and that welcome Canopus had shown me in my previous life...it was night and day.

This cannot go on.

I looked Cyril straight in the eyes. "I can tell you're a kind lord," I said firmly. "And I can tell the Sutherlanders are good people. That's why it hurts so much to see both sides unable to reconcile. I don't know if I'll be able to help, but I ask you to let me try."

A faint, soft smile spread across Cyril's face, one that I'd never seen from him before. "Thank you, Fia. While I'm sure you believe you came to this decision yourself, I still fear that I've had undue influence on you. Allow me to at least guarantee your safety in return. Either I or Kurtis will accompany you at all times. Kurtis has won the citizens' trust, so they should come to trust you if you're seen with him." He stood and looked toward Fabian. "Fabian, I'm counting on you as well to protect Fia if anything happens."

"Yes, sir," he said earnestly.

"So...what am I supposed to *do* here?" I asked. He said something about being a shock to the system, but I had no idea what that entailed.

"Simply walking around with Kurtis or me may be sufficient. The citizens should be shaken enough to start thinking about things just by seeing you, even if you don't do anything in particular."

"I see," I said, nodding.

"Fia..." He gently clasped my hand. "Report back to me in minute detail everything the citizens say and do to you when you're not with me."

"Yes, sir," I said and offered a smile to reassure him.

It didn't seem to assuage his worry. *Being a captain must be rough, always having to look out for your subordinates.*

What to do with my time here, though? "Fabian and I were planning on shopping in town after this, but would it be better if we didn't?"

"No...not at all. If anything, why don't Cyril and I join you?"

And so, the four of us headed for town. Kurtis was relaxed, since he was familiar with the place, but Cyril appeared uneasy.

Hmm. Captain Cyril is the type to overthink things, huh? I swore to myself that I would ease his burden. I would make absolutely sure not to cause him any trouble.

As if he could hear my thoughts, Fabian looked over at me and spoke. "Looking pretty serious, Fia. I'd lighten up and just act like normal, you know? Overthink stuff and you're just asking for trouble."

"R-rude?! I never cause trouble!"

"Of course not," said Kurtis. "From what I can tell, you're a model recruit."

As for Cyril and Fabian, they were oddly silent at that.

Still a bit miffed by their reaction, I entered the town with them. The streets were just as lively as you'd expect from the territory of a duke. People munched on fruit as they walked, talked to their friends, browsed wares—a lively bustle all around. The stores themselves were varied: from grocers selling meat and bread to shops selling household goods and other sundries. Even just window shopping seemed like fun.

That's when I remembered—I proudly turned to the three, pulled out an envelope from my inner pocket with a flourish, and waggled it around in front of their faces. "Look! Spending money! Captain Desmond gave me some as a parting gift!"

"You're not from Desmond's brigade, are you?" asked Kurtis, puzzled. "And yet he gave you a parting gift? How unusual of him," Kurtis said.

"Demond has neither wife nor lover, nor any time with which to spend his oh-so-high salary," said Cyril curtly. "It's not entirely unimaginable for him to give Fia a monetary gift."

"Hmm...what gift should I get Captain Desmond in return?" I asked, hoping to change the topic before Kurtis asked any follow-up questions.

"Maybe a charm to ward off back luck with women," said Cyril. "Better yet, a charm to give him any luck with women in the first place."

"Captain Cyril's suggestion is good," said Kurtis, "but I think Desmond would like food more. He's all about meat, meat, and meat. Get it smoked and it should last until we get back."

My mind ground to a halt, unable to decide between the two captains' wildly different suggestions.

Fabian threw his own suggestion into the mix. "Sutherland is pretty well known for its shells. Why not get a chess set made out of some?"

Gah, stop all suggesting completely different things! Now I'll offend whoever's option I don't pick! There's no way I have enough money to buy all of them either, right?!

Unable to decide, I went to a nearby shop and bought some soy sauce-simmered fish wrapped in a leaf. "One to go, please!"

The shopkeeper started to hand me one with a smile...and went wide-eyed the moment they saw my hair.

"Um...you okay? E-excuse me? Hello?"

"N-no, it's nothing..." they mumbled. They handed me my fish but were clearly averting their gaze.

Yikes. I guess this is that negative reaction to my red hair that Captain Cyril warned me about. But I didn't think it'd be so overt...

I unwrapped the leaf to make the fish easier to eat. "Oh, it's really simmered. I've only seen this fish grilled."

I remembered eating this exact kind of fish in my past life, grilled. It was a species unique to Sutherland's ocean that had a green circular pattern on its side. It was delicious back then.

The shopkeeper looked up with a start and stared—they'd heard me.

H-huh? Uh...did I open my mouth too wide? Oh, maybe there's some sauce stuck to my lips. I casually wiped my lips with the back of my hand, but there was no sauce. *They're practically gonna bore a hole through me with their eyes. To think that the sight of red hair would shock them this much...!*

I turned around to the three men. "This fish is really good! Would you like to try it?"

In unison, they all shook their heads.

Really? Your loss. I dug into the rest of my fish as I went to look at the neighboring store's goods. "Oh, I know this berry juice! This stuff is yummy!"

The shopkeeper heard my voice and looked over with a smile... then he saw my hair and froze right over. *Aaand here we go again.*

The way he froze at the sight of me made me feel like I'd turned into some kinda toothy, drooling monster.

The shopkeeper seemed friendly enough, so I tried directly asking. "Hey, mister, is my red hair really that scary? Or is there something else scary about me that I should know about?"

He remained silent as he looked me over head to toe. When he did finally speak, he sounded frightful. "Young miss, are you... a knight? Or are you a saint dressing up as a knight?"

"I'm a knight. I typically work in the royal capital, but I'm visiting to pay my respects."

Before I knew it, a crowd was forming nearby and beginning to murmur.

"She's a knight? A *knight*? Even with such red hair?"

"There are many shades of red, but the Red of the Great Saint is the red of dawn. That's red, but it ain't *dawn*-red."

"Oh, but it's such a waste of red hair for her to be a knight..."

Just as Cyril had said, the citizens seemed to put some special significance on red hair. But one of the things someone in the crowd had said felt familiar to me.

"The red of dawn..." I murmured to myself. "I remember someone describing my hair like that before..."

But who? People in my past life had described my hair all kinds of ways.

The crowd kept whispering. "N-no, that's definitely the red color of dawn. Has to be."

"No way..."

They stared at my hair in shock.

H-huh? Did they hear me? What's happening?

I fretted, mouth agape, when suddenly something hit my back hard. I turned around to see a boy on the ground—he'd run right into me and fallen over. He was one of the children from the beach earlier.

"Are you okay?" I offered a hand, but the boy just shivered in fear.

"H-h-help! Monsters in the forest! They attacked the others!"

I squatted down to the boy's eye height to try and calm him down. "Monsters, you said?" *I hope they aren't too strong...*

Cyril, Kurtis, and Fabian had been keeping their distance, but they ran up right behind me now. *That's right! I had these three with me to help.*

I tried to look the boy in the face, but he suddenly latched on to me, weeping. Patting his back to calm him down, I spoke as soothingly as I could. "Did you and your friends go to the forest and meet some monsters?"

"Y-y-yeah—*sniff!* The west forest..."

"I see. Do you remember where in the west forest?"

"*Sniff*—mm-hmm..."

"Good boy. I'll let you hold on to me, so can you show me where it was? There are some super-strong knights here that can take care of those monsters lickety-split." I smiled to try and reassure the boy.

The boy raised his face slightly to look at the three knights behind me but soon buried his face back into me. "N-no! Knights don't help Sutherlanders!"

I pretended to not notice the three behind me stir uncomfortably. "That's not true. When I became a knight, I made a promise to always help the weak. All of us did, and we knights never break our promises. You can trust us. Have you ever asked a knight for help and been told no?"

"I...I don't know. I've never tried."

I stood to my feet, lifting the boy up. "I see. But you asked me for help just now, so I'll help you. The knights here with me heard you as well, so they'll help you too."

The boy looked at me, and, without saying a word, he nodded.

Cyril worriedly extended a hand. "Shall I hold the boy for you, Fia? We'll have to slow down if you do."

The boy recoiled with a shriek and clung to me tighter. Dejected, Cyril let his arm droop down.

Kurtis tried talking to the boy next. "Hello. You've probably seen me around before. I'm one of the knights that protects Sutherland, remember? Everyone calls me the Aqua Knight."

"Oh..." The boy seemed to recognize Kurtis a bit.

"We need to hurry," said Kurtis gently. "I'm sure your friends are very scared right now. Will you let me hold you? We'll be able to go faster if I do."

The boy thought for a moment before extending his arms. Just like Cyril had said, the people here accepted Kurtis. I let the boy leave me and latch on to him.

The adults around us, quietly watching up until now, jolted with realization as we prepared to leave.

"Ah! U-um..." stammered someone in the crowd. "The children sometimes enter the forest, but they never venture much farther than the entrance. If it's just some monsters near the forest, we can handle it ourselves!"

"Th-that's right!" another piped up. "We can save the children ourselves! There's no need for you four to bother!"

Despite the danger posed to the children, the citizens still insisted that they didn't want to rely on the knights?

A miserable look crossed Cyril's face before he quickly suppressed it. "Thank you for the offer." he said to the citizens. "But the monsters on the continent have been behaving erratically as of late. Stronger monsters than usual may have appeared near the forest entrance." He stopped to look at the gathered citizens—now all stone-silent—before continuing. "I am First Knight Brigade Captain Cyril. Please, allow me to retrieve your children."

A portion of the citizens seemed surprised to hear his name, whispering among themselves. "The First Knight Brigade Captain? H-he's...the lord?!"

Without waiting for a reply, Cyril turned on his heel and began running toward the forest. Kurtis was about to follow but first paused and turned to the huddled crowd. "We knights are well trained, so you don't need to worry about us. But some of the children might be injured. Could you call for some saints?"

At that, a few people took off running toward the church. Kurtis's words had reassured the citizens, yes, but he'd also given them a task to focus on, in an attempt to foster a sense of comradery. Kurtis knew how to mobilize people.

Not wanting to be left too far behind, I ran all the way to the town's entrance. As luck would have it, a horse was available. I reached the western forest in no time at all—it only took about five minutes to find the children once I reached the forest entrance. Just like the townsfolk said, they didn't travel far.

But why were monsters so close to the outskirts?

The children were safe, thankfully, and had taken refuge in a deep tree hollow. The monsters after them were too big to reach inside the hollow—they were three-meter-long lizard-type monsters called Basilisks. They were B-rank monsters, so usually they were only found far deeper in the forest. Cyril was spot-on about how erratic monster behavior was getting. But there were two Basilisks present, which wasn't exactly a job for only four knights.

Just as I was starting to wonder if we'd bit off more than we could chew, Cyril stepped in, "Fia, I'll leave protecting the boy to you. The three of us are more than enough to handle the two Basilisks."

He was polite about it, but it was clear he thought I'd just get in the way. He wasn't wrong, though. I was the weakest, and somebody needed to look after the boy who'd come to us for help. But could just the three of them really handle a couple of B-rank monsters? Basilisks spit a strong poison, they have tough scales, and they're incredibly nimble. Even if Cyril, strong as he was, had Kurtis and Fabian backing him up...could he really manage?

As I wondered to myself, Cyril cleanly drew his blade. I felt goosebumps all over at once—the air itself had changed around him. *He's so strong!*

Sword in hand, Cyril was suddenly like a totally different being. I'd seen him hold a sword before when he'd fought with Saviz and when he'd faced off against the Flower-Horned Deer, but the aura surrounding him now was something completely different.

He must be the kind of person who adjusts his strength to the situation.

I relaxed, let out a sigh, and checked on the boy who was now worriedly watching the three knights.

"Don't worry," I said. "That knight who just drew his sword is the lord of Sutherland. He's strong. He'll protect us for sure!"

Wordlessly, the boy grabbed my hand and squeezed. I squeezed back, then moved us a safe distance away from the monsters. Basilisks were agile, and I didn't want to risk them getting any ideas about eating delicious kids. I made sure to put the three knights between us and the monsters.

For the record, this is a strategic move! I'm not just using them as meat shields. It's strategy, okay? Yeah. I'm a strategist.

After making sure I'd put enough distance between us and the Basilisks, I checked in on the boy. He wrapped his arms around my waist fearfully.

It's okay, I thought and gently patted him on the arm. He looked up at me, smiled, and loosened his grip a bit.

Still, I wanted to be ready to fight if I had to, so I positioned myself and kept the hilt of my sword close.

The boy's hand trembled in mine. With one hand on the hilt of my blade, I gently patted his hand with the other.

Cyril, Kurtis, and Fabian stared down the monsters at close range. I was worried, but I could tell—even where I was—that the three of them were perfectly calm.

Almost serenely, they stood before two B-rank monsters that would've normally required a team of thirty knights. *I wouldn't expect any less from them.*

The three were positioned a mere ten meters away from the

Basilisks. Cyril—on the left—loosely gripped his silvery sword. He addressed the other two knights without even once looking away from the monsters: "Kurtis. Fabian. Hold back the one on the right for me."

The smaller of the two Basilisks would go to Kurtis and Fabian.

Cyril stared down the Basilisk on the left. Long moments passed in silence. Tension filled the air. A bead of sweat trickled down my back. By nature, Basilisks are hyper-aggressive. They attack their prey on sight. Waiting for an opening was unnatural behavior. Maybe these things were a touch smarter than their brutal brethren.

I couldn't see them being wary of Cyril as he was now, standing still as calm water. You couldn't sense a trace of killing intent or ferocity from him. At first glance, it looked like that earlier strength he'd shown was gone, but he was a top-class fighter. Perhaps hiding such things just showed that he knew what he was doing.

The three knights were wise to keep their distance from the Basilisks. Basilisks could spit poison, but they couldn't just shoot a stream of it. The most effective strategy was to wait for a Basilisk to spit its poison and then close the distance and strike.

Time crawled. The one to lose patience first was the Basilisk that Cyril held in his cool gaze. In just two steps, it dashed five meters forward, spewing poison all the while. The poison spurted forward in a straight line, directly at Cyril's eyes. By the time most people would even notice the Basilisk opening its maw, the poison's already coming at them. The only way to dodge is to predict its attack beforehand.

And Cyril? Cyril just tilted his head and dodged.

"Amazing..." I murmured. I couldn't help it.

I watched in awe as Cyril swiftly closed the distance and thrust his sword into the Basilisk's gaping maw. His sword plunged into the soft flesh of its mouth with little resistance. He heaved the blade out then, just as the monster recoiled onto its hind legs in pain, and Cyril took the opening to swing into its left flank. The sword dug deeply into the Basilisk's hard scales.

From what I could tell, Cyril's swing came at the perfect speed and angle. He plunged his blade in just a bit more, deeper than I even thought possible.

That depth...

Expressionless, he withdrew his blade, spattering bright red blood over the green of the forest. The Basilisk fell dead to the ground.

Yeah, I thought so. Nothing's gonna survive a stab that deep.

Without stopping to shake the blood from his blade, nor even to glance at the fallen Basilisk, he turned toward the remaining monster. Kurtis and Fabian had kept it in check—it hadn't moved a centimeter from its original spot.

Cyril whispered something indistinct, and a blade of wind sliced toward the Basilisk.

"What?!" I exclaimed, and I wasn't the only one surprised— even the Basilisk leapt back.

At the same time, Cyril closed the distance in only a few steps and *woosh*—cut a gash through one of the monster's eyes.

"Greee! Gree, *greeeyaaa*!" The Basilisk roared as it stood on its hind legs in an attempt at intimidation.

Just like he had with the first monster, Cyril swung into its left flank, dug deep into its flesh, and ripped his blade out. The Basilisk's blood sprayed upward. The Basilisk's corpse hit the ground, and its own blood fell onto its body like a gruesome rain.

Cyril swung his sword to shake off the blood and returned it to its sheath without a word.

It was over. Stupefied by his strength, I stared blankly at Cyril.

"O-ow, ow, my hand!" the boy cried.

Oops. Throughout Cyril's fight, I'd been gripping the boy's hand tightly. But even now, I still couldn't break from my trance. I just stared at Cyril.

U-uhh. C-Captain Cyril? How did you...? What did you just...?!

You're just not supposed to approach a Basilisk like he did. Basilisks can aim their poison at their target's eyes with incredible accuracy. Approaching without the support of a mage was insane. And don't even get me started on how he sliced through those scales—scales that are supposed to be nigh-uncuttable. And Basilisks are supposed to have immense physical strength and a powerful, steel-trap bite...not that they ever got a chance to try that on Cyril. Still, they could easily send any ordinary knight flying or chomp a chunk out of them.

One person just can't take on a Basilisk, you know? But Cyril was outlandishly strong. He'd taken two of them out in the snap of a finger, like it was child's play. Honestly, anybody who tried to learn from that fight would be in trouble—they'd have no idea just how deadly Basilisks are. I mean, how they're *supposed* to be. But maybe that was a good thing? Children were present, after all, and there was no need to freak them out. Yeah...there was no need to scare them.

Oh, and I guess Cyril can use wind magic? News to me!

Still holding the boy's hand, I began walking toward the tree hollow where the other children were hiding.

"Nice work," I said to Fabian as he inspected one of the dead Basilisks.

He glanced at me. "I didn't even get to do a thing."

Oh. Right. Such was the problem with teaming with Cyril.

I called out to the children who'd hid in the tree hollow, watching it all unfold. Shakily, they came out of the hole and eyed the two monsters on the ground.

"It's all right," Cyril tried to reassure them. "They won't be getting up anymore."

The children could only manage a wordless nod in response. That's when I noticed a small yellow flower clutched in some of their hands. "Is that a Furi-Furi flower? They can be used to lower fevers, right? Is someone sick?"

The kids looked up, startled, and hid the flowers behind their backs. "N-no! Nobody's sick!"

It was a childish, obvious lie.

"They're a lot like you, Fia," Cyril said.

I pretended not to hear him. *With all due respect, sir, I am an honest girl at heart. I hardly ever lie! It's only sometimes, when I feel that I simply must tell an untruth, that I force myself to deceive. I would never be as childish as an actual child!*

As I voiced my internal monologue to no one, I carefully

checked each child for injuries, finding none. Even better, their fear had subsided enough for them to walk.

"Children sure bounce back fast!" I took the hands of two kids on either side of me. A third child—a small, young girl—came up to me and grabbed the clothes around my belly. I was at a bit of a loss then—I didn't have a third hand, after all—so I looked up at Cyril for help.

Timidly, he stooped over the girl. "Are you tired? Do you want me to carry you back?"

The girl glanced up at him. "I'm too tired to walk," she said. Her voice shook. "But knights are scary. I'm not supposed to go near them."

"I'm not scary. I'm quiet, and I don't get angry."

"You won't get angry...even if I trip in the puddles?"

"We can jump over all the puddles if I'm carrying you. Nobody will get angry, especially not me."

The girl thought for a bit, then let go of my clothes and moved over to Cyril. A soft smile rose to his lips, and I felt happy for him. He was a brave, gentle knight who only wanted to look after his people. If the people of Sutherland knew this side of him, they'd surely come to accept him.

Cyril lifted the girl up onto his shoulders. She laughed, thrilled by her new height. As it turned out, she was rather talkative, pointing out and explaining every little thing she saw.

"That yellow fruit there is really yummy, but you have to pick it while it's green or the birds will eat it first. And! And that big tree over there, it..."

I smiled. *Oh my. This is going better than I thought.* Cyril's polite demeanor was well suited to winning over children. We reached the forest entrance before I knew it.

Some townspeople were waiting for us at the forest entrance, peering in with looks of worry. The instant they saw the children, they cried out with joy, running to meet them. With familiar faces in sight, the children let go of my hands and rushed to them. Cyril didn't even have time to put the girl in his arms down before a townsperson came and snatched her away from him.

"G-get your hands off my daughter!" shouted someone—her mother, presumably.

The girl, surprised to be so suddenly torn away from Cyril's arms, started to cry.

The mother hugged her tightly. "Oh, poor thing. You must've been so scared. Don't worry, Mommy's here now."

Just then, Kurtis started to shout out to the crowd. "Two Basilisks appeared about five minutes from here, but they've been subdued! The children are unharmed, please go notify the ones sent to fetch saints!"

The townspeople knew just how terrifying Basilisks were. I mean, the things could easily swallow children whole, and it usually took tens of knights to defeat such monsters. You'd think these people would be relieved to hear the threat was over, but instead they began whispering amongst themselves.

"D-did he say Basilisks? What's such a horrific monster doing so close to the forest entrance?"

"M-maybe the spirits of the forest are angry? Either way, won't the lord say this happened because we weren't looking after the forest properly? What if he punishes us?"

They all looked over at Cyril, who stiffened. He opened his mouth to say something, but the townspeople around him cut him off.

"What'll it be then?" one of them said. "Are you knights going to punish us even though *you* were the ones who insisted on fighting the Basilisks and putting yourselves in danger?"

"You knights haven't changed in ten years!" Someone else shouted from the crowd. "I'll bet that duke's going to sic his knight goons on us again over some baseless accusations!"

Cyril went wide-eyed. "I've...I've never harmed someone for such a nonsensical reason," he protested. But his voice was nothing more than a whisper, drowned out by the worked-up townspeople.

Kurtis, however, picked up Cyril's words and repeated them louder. "The Duke of Sutherland has not once harmed someone for such a nonsensical reason! Fighting fiendish monsters is a risk all knights are resolved to bear—why, no knight would blame a citizen for needing knights to do such a job! In my time as knight brigade captain of this area, I've never once seen the Duke of Sutherland treat his subjects poorly! On what basis do you speak ill of him?"

"You—all of you—are the ones who hurt us ten years ago over those lies! Our three hundred years of pacifism kept us from fighting back then, but don't think that means we'll just take anything lying down!"

The details of what happened ten years ago were vague, but I knew a ton of townspeople got killed. There was nothing strange about them still holding grudges.

Maybe that's why Cyril raised a hand to stop Kurtis from arguing any further. "I'm sorry if we've caused you trouble," Cyril said quietly. "We were only worried about the children."

The townspeople flinched when he first spoke, expecting some kind of punishment from the highest authority of the land. When they were met instead with his gentle apology, they fell silent.

The person they wanted to berate was Cyril's father, the previous duke.

And Cyril could've shouted back at them, could've argued in so many ways. He could have said that "the past is the past" or admonished them for getting an attitude with the ones who saved their children. But he merely accepted their complaints without a word. He could've had any number of them rounded up and punished, but he didn't.

What would that do but perpetuate the cycle of hate? Cyril was better than that, and so he chose to swallow his complaints. His authority was great, and such power should be used carefully.

Seeing the townspeople taken by surprise at Cyril's kind words, I wanted to shout out at them. "Look, look! This is your lord: kind, caring, gentle!" But why would they believe some knight from far away? They wouldn't accept the truth until they came to the conclusion themselves.

As I stood there, troubled, Cyril gave a quick bow to the silent townsfolk and turned on his heel to leave. The three of us quickly bowed as well and followed after him.

Cyril didn't say a word on the way back to the mansion. He seemed to be deep in thought. Out of consideration, Kurtis didn't say anything either. We all traveled in near silence.

We ate dinner in the banquet hall. Cyril, sitting some distance away, appeared unhappy. He was just a teenager ten years ago when the incident happened—he wasn't even the lord yet—but he still took the townspeople's complaints on his own shoulders. It was the sort of noble thing I'd expect out of Cyril.

Despite my concern for him, I never got a chance to talk to Cyril again before lights out. I thought I'd sleep like a baby after such a hectic day, but to my surprise, I awoke in the middle of the night. That basically never happened to me.

I'm thirsty. I headed for the kitchen. My footsteps echoed down the hallway, I headed up the stairwell to the next floor and immediately bumped into Cyril. A bunch of liquor bottles clinked, held tight in his arms. He'd probably pilfered them from the cellar.

"Are you binge drinking? It's so late..." And there were so many bottles!

He gave a troubled smile. "I have difficulty sleeping at this time every year, so I wind up borrowing the help of alcohol. Unfortunately, a body like mine doesn't get drunk so easily."

Cyril hesitated for a moment. "Ah, Fia..." he continued. "I know it's strange to invite someone this late, but it seems like you're having trouble sleeping as well. Would you like to join me? I have plenty of liquor. It's made from fruit unique to Sutherland."

I didn't miss a beat. "What? Really? I'd love to!"

There were a ton of fruits that only grew in Sutherland, and every single one of them was deliciously sweet. Anybody would be curious about how they'd taste in alcohol, and I was no exception.

I followed Cyril, eventually passing through a large door into what looked to be an office. On the sides of the wide room were lines of tightly packed bookshelves laden with difficult-looking tomes. In the back was a clerical desk completely clear of papers.

This must be Cyril's office.

Continuing in further, another door led to a sort of lounge. Alongside one wall was a cabinet of neatly lined bottles. Wine bottles, as a matter of fact, all attractively colored and uniquely shaped in the way bottles of fruit wine typically were. There was no other liquor to be found.

The floor was lined with empty bottles. *Jeez, Cyril! Ever the heavy drinker...*

He nonchalantly pulled out a chair for me and checked to make sure the door to the hallway was open a smidge—we didn't want anyone to get the wrong idea about two people meeting in the dead of night. In short, he was being a gentleman.

I accepted a beautifully cut glass from him and took a sip. It was, according to him, a liquor made from a yellow fruit produced locally. It was remarkably sweet.

"Ah, delicious..." I muttered, spellbound.

Cyril smiled. Then he downed the strong liquor in his glass in one go.

Now getting a proper look at him, I saw that he was wearing a shirt and trousers. He didn't look like someone who'd crawled into bed once and gotten up like me, still in loungewear. "Have you not slept yet?"

"I...don't feel like sleeping. Not around this time." He wore a complicated expression.

Oh. Of course. That's when it came to me.

The anniversary of the Lament of Sutherland was also the anniversary of his parents' death. The pain of their passing undoubtedly lingered in his heart, resurfacing whenever he went home. Ten years was far too soon for such pain to heal, and yet he bore all that pain today along with the hurt from the townspeople's words.

"What kind of person was your mother?" I asked. Maybe it wasn't appropriate for me to ask, but I believed it was better to express your feelings, not keep them locked inside your heart. At the very least, this was better than bringing up the townspeople from earlier. And while I could've asked about both parents, I got the impression he was closer with his mother.

Cyril studied my face for a few moments, deep in thought, and then looked to my red hair. "Yes, well...Mother was beautiful. And she was a saint too...with the same red hair as the Great Saint herself."

He slunk back into his seat and squeezed his glass. Little by little, he began to open up about his mother.

A Tale of the
Secret
Saint

Cyril, Captain of the First Knight Brigade

MY MOTHER WAS BEAUTIFUL. Even without her red hair—hair as red as the legendary Great Saint—she would still be just as beautiful. And she was a high-ranking saint, which allowed her to marry into a prominent ducal family.

From the moment I was born, I had a right to the throne. As such, I was assigned many instructors and was taught a wide breadth of things from a young age. Above all, though, I was made to study saints. From as far back as I could remember, the fact that the royal family and the nobles existed to protect the saints was drilled into me. I was taught that the saints were the foundation of our kingdom and protecting them maintained its very existence. But of all my saint-related studies, we spent the most time covering the Great Saint who lived three hundred years ago.

The legend who sealed away the demon king, the one and only Great Saint.

That performer of impossible feats, the beautiful and noble Great Saint.

The icon whose hair was the color of dawn and her eyes the color of wheat—the very symbol of abundance.

Like most upper nobility, a portrait of her hung in our home. She stood in that image, her vivid red hair swaying in the wind as she stared straight into my soul with her defiant golden eyes. She was so utterly beautiful...but because of that beauty, my mother— with her similar red hair—was so arrogant.

I was raised by a wet nurse, as many high-ranking noble children were. I wasn't allowed to dine with my parents as a child, and I rarely ever saw my mother. Occasionally, I would pass her in the hallway or garden, but she'd always walk past as though she didn't see me. Still, I would turn and watch until she slipped out of sight, burning the image of her beautiful red hair into my mind.

My fifth birthday was the first time I was allowed to join my parents for dinner. When they asked me what I wanted for my birthday, I naively asked for a little brother. I had a close friendship with Saviz, the second prince, who was the same age as me. I longed to have a relationship like the one he had with the first prince.

Upon hearing this, my mother frowned. "Absurd. I've endured more than enough, giving birth to you for the sake of this measly ducal family. We're not even royalty, so what good is having a spare? If something happened to you, so be it, this household might as well die off."

She wiped the corners of her mouth with a napkin, then crudely tossed it onto the table. "We saints are nothing but disposable to you all. Those who wed into royal blood can only bear boys. My red hair is doomed to fade away, inherited by no one.

Just look at you and your filthy gray hair, Cyril. You don't take after me in the slightest. If I were to bear another child, it'd just be another filthy gray-haired boy like you. Who could possibly want such a thing?"

That was the first time I'd spoken more than a greeting with my mother. Until then, I still clung to the belief that she loved me—that she was the beautiful, kind, and caring mother I had always imagined. All the more reason her harsh words took me by such surprise. I was at a loss for what to say.

She looked at me like I was a revolting stain on a fine dress. "Can you not even muster a reply? I suppose a ducal family's education *would* amount to nothing. Oh, why am I trapped here, stuck being your mother?! I am the greatest of the saints! I should've been queen!"

With that, my mother stood from her seat and swept out of the room, leaving a mountain of food untouched on her plate. I couldn't understand what had happened. Had I said something to anger her? I looked to my father for help.

My father looked down at me impassively. "Cyril, when you have finished eating, go apologize to your mother. After that, study until you have the bare minimum of common sense."

Ashamed, I hung my head.

My father must be right, I thought. I'd lacked common sense and wasn't even aware of it. I was ashamed from the bottom of my heart to have believed the praise of my instructors. I wasn't smart for a five-year-old child. They were just giving me empty praise because I was the son of a duke.

In the end, I wasn't granted an audience with my mother. I never got to apologize.

That night, our butler came to my room and begged my forgiveness. "Forgive me, I bear all responsibility for what transpired. I assumed it too early to tell you of the relationship between His Majesty the King and His Grace the Duke, as well as Her Grace the duchess."

The butler was quite competent, so I assumed he had his reasons for withholding information...reasons that I was soon to learn.

He began to explain about my family. From him, I learned one fact known to many, another fact known only to the Sutherland family, and finally the reason for my mother's reaction.

Though it was never made public, my mother was the most powerful saint of the time. In other words, she *should* have been married to the king. But it was an unspoken rule among the men of the royal family and their blood relatives that they should marry before turning thirty. On the other hand, saints couldn't marry until they were seventeen. When my mother was fifteen, the king himself was twenty-eight...and in a hurry to marry. With her unavailable, the Church and the king's retainers arranged for the second-most powerful saint to become queen instead—my mother's older sister.

The most powerful saint always becomes the queen—this ironclad rule helps to maintain the authority of the kingdom. To keep that rule in place, the king's loyal retainers altered the rankings of the powerful saints. My mother was downgraded to the *second* most powerful, and her sister was moved up to her former position.

Denied her rightful position, my proud mother felt slighted. Even marrying my father, a former member of the royal family, didn't help. Being the second-most important woman in the kingdom was no consolation for losing the chance to be queen. Not once did she take pride in marrying my father, the most prominent duke, nor did she ever in her life come to terms with the injustice of her lowered rank.

Father pitied my mother. As a former member of the royal family, he was made to learn about saints even more strictly than I was. He was taught that saints were sacred and meant to be treated with utmost respect. When the mightiest saint, the one most truly deserving of veneration, was denied her royal destiny... guilt took hold of him.

To my mother, my father wasn't a husband but a shield meant to protect her. My father agreed with this view.

Thus ended the butler's explanation.

Hearing it, I became painfully aware of my own ignorance. Once again, I was deeply ashamed. I wasn't supposed to treat my mother like a mother, you see. No, she deserved only the reverence due to all saints. I couldn't expect a mother-child relationship from her. She may have given birth to me, but that fact meant nothing to her. I never should have expected it to.

From that point on, I strove to treat this holy saint gracing our home with the proper respect she deserved. I always acted with decorum and spoke courteously to her. Perhaps thanks to my meticulous efforts, she never rebuked me again.

It pleased me to know that I kept her in good spirits, but my heart ached whenever I saw a normal and harmonious mother-child pair. I grew accustomed to that ache, though. The greatest of saints graced my home. What more could I wish for?

When I turned ten, I began regularly traveling between the royal capital and the territory. My father allowed me to use his title of earl as my own courtesy title, allowing me to enter the Royal Castle without much trouble—father had many titles of his own, after all.

Mother hated the royal capital and stayed home in our own territory. I imagined she didn't want to see everything that would have been hers as queen. Periodically, I would check in on her to see if she needed anything. She never responded. Whenever I spoke to her, she didn't meet my eye—she'd merely sip her tea, admire the flowers, and continue whatever she was preoccupied with. I might as well not have existed.

She was your prototypical saint, through and through. Prideful and always placing her own desires first, she believed herself to be above all others and demanded to be treated as such. For that reason, she loathed the people of Sutherland.

The majority of Sutherland's people were former islanders. You could recognize their characteristics at a glance...and Mother abhorred their appearance. Their skin was dark brown and their hair dark blue...both of which my mother called filthy. Their webbed fingers—evolved from years of ocean life—my mother called a curse. She often compared them unfavorably to the many noble-born maids and butlers she called in from the capital, concluding that the Sutherland people were uncultured and vulgar. To her, all people who were born inland were superior. The fact that she had to live around these islanders who, in her mind, didn't look right...she saw it as an affront.

Furthermore—for better or worse—the saints in Sutherland weren't very saintlike at all. The majority of them were former islanders and were neither arrogant nor selfish. Unfortunately, their saint powers were weak—*much* weaker than my mother's. And so, whenever there was a serious injury or illness, the people of Sutherland ran to my mother to ask for help...only for her to refuse them.

I recall a young girl who suffered terrible burns. Her father came begging for help. My mother cut him off. "You islanders and your disgusting dialect!" she told him. "I can't make sense of a single word you're saying!" He was turned away.

I recall a man in his thirties who came to her carrying his bloodied father on his back. He had been attacked by a monster. She didn't even speak to the man—her butler informed him that she was busy. Mother had tea to drink and flowers to admire.

Occasionally, she would heal someone, seemingly on a whim, and earn their heartfelt gratitude. But the few she healed were mostly nobility who traveled from afar. Not one of them were former islanders.

Despite the way she treated them, the Sutherlanders revered my mother. But why? We nobles are taught from a young age to honor the superiority of the saints, yes, but common folk receive no such education. I thought it strange at the time. I knew the people were devout worshippers of the Great Saint, but was that alone enough for them to overlook my mother's petty cruelties?

But then, their adoration of my mother came to an end. It all began with a single tree.

Before our mansion lay a wide courtyard, and in the middle of that courtyard stood a magnificent tree. It towered over thirty meters tall and was lush with freely growing branches. One couldn't help but notice it when visiting as, from the entrance of the gate, it obscured the majority of the mansion. This tree that so dominated the courtyard was planted three hundred years ago by the Great Saint, together with the people of the land, to commemorate her visit. Eventually, it grew large enough that it became a sort of landmark for the mansion.

Once a year, the people held a celebration in memory of the Great Saint's visit. The courtyard was opened to the public at that time, allowing the townspeople to gather around the tree. They'd offer up dances and show appreciation for the latest year of safety they had received.

My mother didn't show any particular interest in the tree for a long while...until she learned it was planted by the Great Saint.

The people were worshipping something created by someone superior to her, and she found that positively unbearable.

She had the tree cut down. Then she ordered the wood made into a set of chairs and a table, both of which she kept in the courtyard and used for her teatime.

To her, it may have just been any old tree, but to the people, it was a symbol of the Great Saint herself. After she had the tree cut down, the people began openly avoiding her at every turn. Whenever she went on an outing, the people made themselves scarce. No longer did anyone seek healing from her.

This angered my mother. A powerful saint like her should be sought out, respected and venerated, she thought, and so her distaste for the people grew. A fissure had formed between the people and their once-venerated saint.

That was when the accident happened.

On that fateful day, my mother went to the cape in search of a rare herb. From atop a steep cliff facing the ocean, she barked orders at a few Sutherlanders.

"Not that one! Climb lower. Grab the one right at your feet."

She stood, looking over the very edge of the cliff as she shouted commands at the ones picking herbs with their backs to the cliff's edge. A hand reached out and touched her arm.

"Duchess, it's dangerous to be so far forward. Please ba—"

But the person never got to finish their words. My mother smacked their hand away. "Do not touch me with your lowborn hands! Agh, how filthy! There is a world of difference between us, do you understand?! You all have no right to address me, much less touch me! No matter what reason you might give, no matter what situation arises, you lowborns are to never lay your grimy paws on me! The next of you to do so will lose the hand that offended me! Your family will be punished for the next three generations! If you understand, then get away from me!"

At that very moment, a strong gust of wind hit her. She lost her footing and plummeted from the cliff. She didn't surface, perhaps due to the weight of her extravagant dress. The servants and knights in attendance frantically plunged into the ocean after her, but the currents were too fast and the waters too murky from the previous day's rain.

Her body was never found.

By chance, my father was passing by and saw the servants and knights desperately fighting against the waves, as well as the citizens doing nothing, only watching from above. A knight surfaced from the ocean and reported that they'd failed to find the duchess.

My father struck him. "How could you fools let our heavenly saint drown right under your nose?!"

He looked out toward the sea from the cliff. Parts of the expansive blue ocean before him appeared murky, but not a scrap of dress nor a single figure could be seen. The duchess was gone from this world.

Unsteadily, he turned around, drew out the sword at his hip...and began to attack the townspeople around him. "Why did none of you try to help Her Grace?! She was the second-greatest saint of our Kingdom, the foundation of our society!

All of you shall repent with your lives—every single one of your kind!"

My father ordered his knights to kill the citizens. A conflict between the knights and the people followed and lasted for two days. My father tragically lost his life during the fighting, but at least his death put an end to it.

"My parents' relationship was twisted until the end," I said, sighing. "I doubt an outsider could truly ever understand them. Father always felt guilty that mother wasn't properly acknowledged as the Kingdom's greatest saint." The feelings and emotions I'd locked away deep within my heart were beginning to resurface, like sediment stirring at the bottom of a pool.

"I wasn't there myself," I continued. "I can only try to understand what happened through secondhand information. Even so, I think the fault lies with my parents. But the Kingdom's already passed down a verdict on the matter, and so I cannot say such a thing." I spoke so much more carelessly than usual, so much more *truthfully*. "No matter how guilty I feel, my position doesn't allow me to contradict the verdict and apologize..."

Fia tilted her head thoughtfully. "I see...because if you apologized, it'd be like admitting guilt on the part of the late duke and his knights. The current verdict from the kingdom considers both sides equally guilty, and they didn't punish either. Maintaining that balance allows the least loss."

I was lost for words. Fia was sharp. She wasn't all there some of the time—perhaps most of the time—but when it truly mattered, she grasped the essence of things.

She made a face I couldn't quite put a finger on and bit her lip. "That's...a sad story. I feel like if just one thing leading up to that incident were changed, then things would have played out differently," she muttered, gazing at her hands, spreading her fingers. "Really, I don't see how being a saint is any different from any other job."

"What do you mean?" I was genuinely taken by surprise. Only those granted power by God could become saints. To call it a mere occupation like any other was...blasphemous.

"I meant exactly what I said. Just as a good cook becomes a chef, those who can use healing magic become saints. The idea that they should be put on some high pedestal for their talents, that's the main problem."

"Ah, right, you *did* have a fairly unique perspective on saints..." I said, putting my glass on the table and turning to face Fia directly. "You were rather intoxicated when you said it, so you might not remember, but you once gave your opinion on how saints should behave while I was present. You said, 'Saints aren't goddesses, distant and fickle with their gifts. They are the shield of the knights.' I felt like my heart had been pierced the moment I heard those words."

Having recounted the moment, the emotions I'd felt then bubbled up once more, stirring my heart. I balled my hand into a fist to try and keep myself collected. "What I'm about to tell you isn't exactly fair to you, Fia...but I believe what people say changes depending on their circumstances. You could say what you said just now—and what you said that night, for that matter—because you're a knight. If you were a saint, on the other hand, you'd never say such a thing."

Fia didn't respond.

Countless times have I recalled the night Fia spoke those words that so shook me. The purpose of those words, how she could think in such a way, why she would even say such things, I've considered it all. My conclusion boiled down to one thing: Fia was not a saint.

It was her own ideals and desires as a knight that led her to say that the saints are the shield of the knights, and once I decided on that explanation, I thought no further of it. Or perhaps I'd merely hit a block and moved on.

People were shaped by their circumstances and environment. I myself grew accustomed to acting politely in the presence of my mother, and, before I knew it, I became endlessly polite to *everyone*. I was incapable of acting any other way.

"Fia, I...understand what I said isn't fair to you," I said. "It's not your fault that you aren't a saint."

Fia looked me straight in the eyes. With a mysterious expression I couldn't quite place, she gracefully replied, "Perhaps. But if I were a saint, my opinion wouldn't change."

Something about those words struck a chord with me. *Maybe it wouldn't,* I thought. For whatever reason, I believed her. I believed she really might say the same things if she was a saint.

The moment I came to that conclusion, the filth I'd let pool in the depths of my heart began to slowly clear a little. Feeling my burdens lighten, I dressed my true feelings as a joke. "Heh. I'm... glad you aren't a saint. If you had a saint's power and could still say such things, I'd be forced to drop to my knees and become your follower."

It was all hypothetical, but she looked greatly troubled by that. "A-absolutely not! I can't have a follower like you! Your presence would only get in the way of my plans to find a lover and marry in the future!"

"Ha ha! If I were your follower, I'd be more than happy to screen a lover for you."

"N-no way! People use their own criteria to screen others, right?! If you screened people, nobody would meet your standards!"

Seeing her so strongly argue against the idea, I broke into laughter. *Fia really is rather saintly, isn't she?* This time of year always left me in a depressive, dreary mood, but...today I was laughing.

Fia had the power to save the hearts of others. Was this not a power rivaling that of a saint? She frowned as I smiled happily. Gazing at her, I took my first pleasant sip of alcohol in a long time.

The Visit to Sutherland Part 2

I WOKE UP THE NEXT DAY feeling conflicted. I'd guessed that Cyril's mother was a saint, but hearing she was as arrogant as the other saints of this time came as a shock. Had all my hard work been for nothing? I thought I'd tried my hardest in my past life to teach the younger saints that they were the shield of the knights. Sure, I'd died younger than I'd expected to, but hadn't anyone carried out my will? Did my personal knight Canopus stand back and do nothing as the concept of the saints was twisted beyond recognition? Or was the change a gradual process over the past three hundred years, something beyond his control?

Which reminded me—I still needed to visit his grave. *Oh, right! Canopus loved this land and its people. His grave* has *to be in Sutherland somewhere! And since it's me we're talking about, it should be a cinch to find it!*

Canopus was my personal knight. It would be no exaggeration to say I had spent more time with him than with anyone else in my previous life, so of course I knew him better than anyone else. I knew all the places he held close to his heart, so—obviously—it would be easy to find his grave.

Or so I thought. Oh, how naive I was...

Four hours later, I looked back on how stupid I'd been as I panted like a dog, exhausted, still no closer in my search. I was stumped. I checked everywhere he might have put his grave—from the courtyard of the mansion to a cape that overlooked the ocean—only to come up empty-handed.

What the...? I thought I understood him so well! And who would I even ask about a three-hundred-year-old grave?! What can I do?

Sighing, I sat down on a cliff and looked out at the ocean. Before me stretched an endless field of blue, its waves rising and falling over the salty smell of its surface. This was the ocean of Sutherland that Canopus so dearly loved, and further south of it lay the island he was born on.

"Canopus, it took me a while, but I've finally come to see the ocean you loved," I whispered to no one in particular. I brushed aside my wind-swept hair. "It's serene, as though it were one with the sky."

"Fia? Are you talking to someone I can't see? Or were you just talking to yourself?" Yeesh...whoever was speaking from behind sure had bad timing.

One, two, three—I counted to compose myself before turning around. "Oh, Captain Cyril! I wasn't talking to myself, exactly, but more like an acquaintance of mine? They passed away quite a while ago, but they loved this land. I figured they probably returned here to rest. I thought it'd be nice if they were actually with me, so I just started talking to myself like they were."

"Ah. I see." He moved to stand by my side and looked out at the blue ocean. "From that point of view, couldn't you say that my mother is at rest in the ocean? We...never did find her body, after all. Odds are that she's sleeping in the depths even now."

"Captain..." I glanced up at Cyril. He wore a wistful, reminiscent look.

"Fia, I want to run something by you, and I want to hear what you think—what you honestly think—as a friend. I couldn't save my parents. For ten long years, I've thought it all over, but even now I still don't know what I should've done...or what to do now for the people of Sutherland." His gaze didn't move from the ocean as he spoke.

He continued. "I've long believed that it's my responsibility to fix the damage my family has done. By governing this land, by understanding its people, and by healing their wounds, I...I really did believe that I could make up for our wrongdoing all those years ago. But perhaps I'm not even meant to govern this land. I've tried so much over the past ten years, but my relationship with the people hasn't improved one bit. I can't help these people, Fia... Can I?" His voice was calm and composed, but his eyes stubbornly refused to look away from the ocean. I thought it strange that the ever prim and proper Cyril wasn't meeting my eyes.

That's when I noticed the slight tremble in his balled fists. He hadn't just thought this up today or yesterday—no, this was a conclusion he'd reached after years of consideration. He couldn't publicly acknowledge the faults of his parents, not with his position to worry about, but he believed he could at least try and improve things to make up for it.

And the people didn't care for any of his efforts.

With his kindness and strong sense of responsibility, he probably felt guilt for all the pain his family had caused the Sutherlanders. He believed that stepping down as lord could alleviate some of that pain.

"Captain Cyril, what your parents did here when they governed this land, and what you do now that you govern, are two completely different things."

At that, Cyril took a deep breath. Purposefully looking away from him, I watched the ocean waves rise, collapse into foam, and rise again. "Some things have no answers. People do...unexplainable things. And when they do, you can think about their actions for a lifetime and still not understand why. I've tried it myself and found no explanations."

I'll never understand why my brothers left me for dead in the Demon Lord's castle. Rise, fall, foam. *Never...*

"But I have no way of fully knowing the lives they led," I said. "And I'll never completely understand how they thought. No matter how many times I think about it, it just...won't give me any answers."

"Fia...?" My words must have sounded cryptic to him. He looked concerned.

I smiled. "That's why I decided to just not think about it! It's not easy. I mean, what happened largely defines who I am today. But what's the point in being held back by something I'll never understand? I can still move forward as I am now. I can still smile, even."

I looked up at him. "You're very kind, Captain Cyril. But what would you be if you hadn't gone through what happened with your parents? No way of knowing, you know? And I like this Captain Cyril."

His eyes shot wide at this. I continued. "There might be some people out there you can't help. There might even be some people who don't want the help you offer. Even so, you try your best to help them, and that's wonderful. If I lived in Sutherland, I would want someone like you as my lord."

Shocked, Cyril opened his mouth to say something. But no words came out, so he closed it again.

I turned away from the ocean and faced him directly. "The people here haven't been able to move on. I know that hurts. But it'll be okay, I'm sure of it. Your kindness will get through to them in the end."

For a brief while, his shocked expression lingered. Eventually, however, he smiled. Then he began, quietly, to laugh. "Ha ha ha. Your world is so simple it's beautiful... It's—ha—enchanting!"

After continuing to giggle for some time, he made this lovely smile, as if he'd stepped out of a dark prison into the sun. "I'm not sure what you're basing your words on, but I think I want to see that beautiful world of yours. Yes...this is no time to be grumbling over the past. Doing all that I can to help the people, making sure that someday we see eye to eye... Day by day, I can work at this. Thank you, Fia. I feel better after talking with you."

"You're welcome?" I didn't quite understand why he was so happy, but his gratitude was nice to hear regardless.

The two of us gazed out over the ocean for some time. Eventually, Cyril broke the silence. "Why did you come to this cape anyway? To see the sea?"

"Umm, well, I was looking for the grave of the Blue Knight so I could offer a prayer or something."

"Ohh, I see. You did show some interest in the Blue Knight when I told you my last name. Unfortunately, I've never heard anything about his grave being in Sutherland."

"What, really?!" I exclaimed, distraught. *Sutherland isn't Canopus's resting place?! Then where in the world is it?!*

I let my shoulders go slack and looked over at Cyril. "Ugh. I guess that means there's no point in searching any more. So, what about you, Captain? Did you come here just to gaze at the sea?"

"No, although it seems that's what I ended up doing. I meant to come looking for you. You missed lunch."

"Huh? Wha—I'm so sorry I caused you trouble! But I'm fine missing a meal, you know?"

As though admonishing a child, Cyril frowned and lightly bonked me on the head. "What are you saying? You're still growing—you need to eat! Besides, dinner's going to be on the lighter side today, so you'll regret missing lunch."

"It will?" A thought crossed my mind, then. "Oh, don't tell me, the mansion ran out of food because the knights ate way more than you expected?"

He gave me an exasperated look. "Do you think my pantry is so meager that it could only hold a few days' worth of food for a mere hundred knights? No—dinner is light because there's a festival for the anniversary of the Great Saint's visit tomorrow. The festival begins at sunrise, so we'll be eating an early, modest dinner. We'll also be sleeping earlier than usual, in order to be up before dawn."

"Th-th-the festival for the anniversary of the Great Saint's visit?!" I blurted. *There's such a thing?! Does that mean...they've been doing it for three hundred years now?! C-Canopus, you dummy! Why didn't you stop them?!*

Then again, people needed entertainment, and something like the Great Saint's visit was fairly easy to get behind. I could see why it was made a thing, but wasn't it in bad taste to continue the festivals after I'd died...?

Man... I can just see it now. After three hundred years, no way every single detail about me would be passed down correctly. What if they thought I was actually super out of shape, or a bumbling idiot, or who knows what else?!

Fraught with worry, I followed Cyril back to his mansion.

Unlike when I left in the early morning, the courtyard was open and full of citizens preparing for the festival. Their preparations were centered around the stump in the middle of the courtyard.

"Oh, right, it was an adela tree, wasn't it?" I muttered. "It must've been really big." I could only imagine the size of the thing, given the massiveness of the stump.

Cyril looked down at me doubtfully. "How did you know it was an adela tree? I mentioned it was cut down last night, but I'm pretty sure I never spoke of its type."

"Uh, I-I...love trees? Y-yeah! I can tell trees apart just by looking at their stump!"

"Oh, really?" He didn't sound convinced.

I averted my gaze, pretending nothing was unusual. *Crud. Captain Cyril's too sharp. I better keep my mouth shut from now on.*

Biting my tongue, I followed Cyril to the dining hall.

After scarfing down lunch, I left for the courtyard and began helping the townspeople prepare. I guess it was tradition for knights to help with festival preparations—many had already set to work and knew what to do. The townspeople were as reserved toward us as ever, but they didn't object to our presence, muttering the bare minimum needed to get by with us.

Heh heh. Festivals are nice. They loosen people up, you know? Give even a rocky relationship like the one between us and the townspeople a chance to heal.

Even after the tree—the Great Saint's Tree, they called it—was cut down, the people continued to use the stump as the center of festivities, reserving an extensive space around it for events. They decorated the stump in a variety of vibrant cloths.

Evening arrived, and we were mostly done with our preparations. Knights began setting up flag stands here and there in the courtyard, surrounding the Great Saint's Tree with fluttering cloth. I watched, curious. Soon enough, they'd hoisted the flag of the Náv Kingdom.

"Huh? What're they doing?" I asked. Our flag, a black dragon over a red base, was a complete mismatch to the merry mood of the festival.

Fabian answered from beside me. "Oh, that? The townspeople let us use our flag for the festival. Normally, red is a forbidden color, but we still use it for the flag. You see, the red on the flag is said to be the exact same red as the Great Saint's hair. The festival is in her honor, and so they allow us to raise the flag in her name."

"Ohhh." Saviz had said something like that, about how the red on the flag was the color of my hair. He even took me all the way to the highest floor of the castle just to compare them. I denied it by insisting that red has a ton of shades, but he said he was sure it was the same shade.

I guess the red of the flag and my hair really were the same color, then. Ha—what a weird coincidence.

With preparations done, I raced for the dining room and wolfed down my dinner. *The festival starts at sunrise tomorrow, so I'll need to get up while it's still dark. I need to fall asleep...quickly!*

And sure enough, I was out like a light.

When I woke to the sound of my roommates getting dressed, I got started at once. I rushed to get ready and made my way to the courtyard. A ton of knights and citizens had gathered—things were already looking lively. I slipped into the line of knights and waited for things to kick off.

Finally, a beam of light peered over the horizon and signaled the beginning of the festival. Cyril, the lord, laid an adela branch with a red flower on the old tree's stump before everyone. The moment he bowed, we all did the same. We held our bows for a while when I suddenly heard sobbing. I looked up in surprise to see a number of citizens weeping with their hands over their faces.

"Th-thank you, oh Great Saint."

"Please visit again!"

A feeling of warmth filling my chest, I bowed again, deeply. *Thank you. I'm honored to receive such love after only one visit.*

I thanked the people of this land from the bottom of my heart and prayed they would lead happy, healthy lives.

The festival continued without pause, the next event being the offering of dance to the Great Saint. The earlier solemn mood was now gone, and everyone was free to celebrate as they pleased. Half of the knights took to visiting the stands, the quickest of us already tearing into some grub. I stayed with the citizens, taking a seat on the rug laid out before the stage, ready for the dancing to start. There was still some time left before it began, so I waited, vacant minded, when I heard a couple of citizens behind me talking.

"Whenever the adela flowers bloom, I always get my hopes up thinking the Great Saint might visit."

"Me too. It'd be nice to meet her, if only just once."

I fought the urge to turn around then and there. *H-huh?*

Cyril said there hadn't been any other Great Saints, which meant they had to be talking about my past life. But I'd died three hundred years ago! I was a saint, not some immortal monster!

There was no way I could live for three hundred years...so why were they still waiting for me?

Interested in their conversation, I pricked up my ears. One of them giggled. "I heard when the Great Saint visited Sutherland her dress and hair were all disheveled. Heh heh! Even when she's a mess, a visit from her is a wonder!"

W-wait, wait, wait! You said it like a compliment, but that sounded like a diss? I guess the worries I'd had when I first learned about the festival were warranted. Either information was passed down incorrectly or only the funnier bits stuck around.

I slumped my shoulders, saddened, though I still listened to the two just in case they let out a genuine compliment. No such luck—they moved on from my past life and started talking about last night's dinner.

O-oh. I see. Of course, last night's dinner would take precedence over some ancient story about the Great Saint. No surprise there, I thought, dejected. Just then, instruments began to play. It was time for the dance to start.

My mood picked up the moment the music reached my ears. I sat on the edge of my seat, eager, as ten or so beautifully dressed women appeared, dancing in tune with the bells. The many-colored fabrics they wore were dazzlingly beautiful, and they were fun to watch, but...

"Hmm. I thought they'd begin with some kids first, but I guess they're going all out from the beginning."

Overhearing my muttering to myself, the woman sitting next to me eyed my hair and gave me an explanation. "When the

Great Saint visited this land, we were unable to show her more than a single dance. That's why we have a tradition of offering up the most important dance first."

"Oh, really? Ah, wait, no! I couldn't help it! I really was looking forward to seeing everyone dance, okay? I just got so tired I fell asleep! B-but the children were cute, so I felt really welcomed!" I blurted, trying to make excuses.

Wait, um…I probably shouldn't make excuses to a random person about something that literally happened a lifetime ago. But it was all too late. The citizens around me stared in shock. *Yeah. I'd be creeped out too if some red-haired knight started saying strange things.*

"A-about what you said just now… How did you know the Great Saint only saw the children dance?"

"Look at that red hair. Maybe it's her after all?"

"Hair the color of dawn and golden eyes. The same as the Great Saint…"

"It's her…!"

Everyone around me started whispering, especially about my hair. What I said just now had likely appalled them, but what was with the comments about my hair? Or wait, did it have to do with that thing Cyril mentioned about the people taking offense at the color of my hair?! People generally welcomed redheads in Sutherland—it reminded them of the Great Saint—but those old enough to remember the Lament of Sutherland often associated it with the cruel duchess instead.

A quick look around told me everyone present was an adult… which meant my red hair was probably dredging up memories of the duchess from ten years ago. They were probably whispering to each other even now. Stuff like "Look, another red-haired woman is causing trouble again! Listen to all the weird stuff she's saying!"

I didn't want to trample on their feelings any further, so I tried just sitting quietly for a bit and then nonchalantly moving my gaze back toward the stage. But the whispers around me didn't cease. In fact, they grew louder.

I began to worry what could possibly be wrong when a well-built man sitting near me timidly asked, "Miss, can you tell what kind of dance they're doing onstage?"

"Hmm..." I focused on the movements of the dancers. "From the way they're fluttering playfully, you'd think they look like jellyfish, but they're actually dancing like dolphins! Heh heh! That was a nice trick question, but you can't fool me!"

My smug answer was met with even more looks of shock.

"But...but how...? Their movements look nothing like a dolphin's!"

"It's true, then...it must be her..."

A number of people leapt to their feet. The spectator seats began to buzz with excitement. The dancers weren't the center of attention anymore.

Kurtis, catching wind of the clamor, came running over. He looked surprised to see that I was the cause of the commotion. "Fia, what happened? Everyone's in uproar, and it's all around you?"

Uproar was a good way of putting it, yeah. The first dance had finished, but things were getting restless enough that the next dance hadn't started. Everyone was standing up in the spectator seats, all whispering and crowding around me.

I was in tears. "I-I-I don't know! Somebody asked me to guess what the dance was like, and I said dolphin and now something's wrong!"

"Huh? Just from that?" He made a face at me, tilting his head to the side all exaggerated-like.

"Yeah, just from that! Was it a rude thing to say in Sutherland or something?!"

"Not that I know of. I was watching from a distance away, but weren't they imitating jellyfish? Maybe everyone's just exasperated over how totally, massively wrong you were?"

"C-Captain Kurtis! Does this look like they're exasperated to you?!" I protested, glaring up at him.

"It was a joke," he said, trying to reassure me with a smile and discreetly moving to hide me behind his back. He looked around at everyone and spoke in a calm voice. "I am Kurtis, captain of the Thirteenth Knight Brigade that has jurisdiction over this land. We knights were looking forward to celebrating the anniversary of the Great Saint's visit with everyone. I apologize if my fellow knight has done something rude."

Cyril had mentioned before that the people of Sutherland accepted Kurtis. Sure enough, his words seemed to make the people relax, and one of them replied, "A-ah, no, she hasn't done anything wrong. W-we were just wondering who this young lady here was..."

"Y-yeah," another added. "Who's this young lady with red hair like the dawn?"

"This is Fia, a new knight recruit in our Kingdom," Kurtis answered.

The citizens exchanged wary looks and began to talk amongst themselves—

"A knight. A knight, huh?"

"Wait, think about it. The Great Saint trusts knights and values them highly."

"Yeah, and isn't it a knight's job to protect the country and its people? That does sound like something the Great Saint would do."

—and as the commotion continued, an elderly man stepped forward from the crowd.

"It's nice to meet you, young lady. I am Radek, chief of the former islander people," he said and bowed.

"It is an honor to make your acquaintance. I am Fia Ruud of the First Knight Brigade." I introduced myself to Radek and bowed. It appeared he and Kurtis were already acquainted, as they only exchanged a brief nod.

His wrinkled face shifted into a wide smile as he gestured for us to sit on the rug. "Why don't we sit down? Standing for a long time is difficult at my age."

The three of us did just that, the curious people gathering around us. Radek looked at my hair, astonishment plain on his face. "That's some lovely red hair you have there. We only know of it through word of mouth, but Her Holiness the legendary Great Saint was said to have a similar vibrant red. It's beautiful."

"Thank you very much, although I've heard that the late duchess also had red hair," I replied. "In fact, red hair isn't all that uncommon in the royal capital."

Softly, he replied, "I saw the late duchess's hair myself, but it was more of an orange-tinted red. Yours is vibrant. Even on all the trips I took to the royal capital on business, I only ever saw amber-red and brown-red hair, none of it in that incredible crimson you have."

"Is that so?" Maybe he was right. I'd never really given a lot of attention to other people's red hair, so I couldn't fully deny the possibility that my hair color was unique.

The old man gave a hearty laugh and held out the adela branch in his hand. "Ha! Most high-ranking saints insist their hair is as red as the Great Saints, but your hair truly is that color, and you don't seem to care at all. Here. I couldn't protect the adela tree that the Great Saint planted, but I was able to obtain a branch before it was cut down, and I grew another tree from it. That tree's grown big enough now to sprout a branch like this."

I looked at the red flower that grew on the branch and smiled. "Wow, thank you."

He smiled as well. "The folks here said you seemed to know a lot about Sutherland. Are you acquainted with a local? What made you think the first dance was based on a dolphin?"

"I'm not quite acquainted with anyone so much as...interested, I suppose, in the Blue Knight who was Sutherland's lord long ago.

I've been wanting to visit the ocean and town here for a while now because of that. As for the dolphin thing...uh, well, there's not much difference between dolphins and jellyfish, is there? So, y'know, I kinda confused the two..." The moment I said those words, the people who were listening in on us let out a gasp. They stared at me as though unable to believe their eyes.

I fidgeted uncomfortably and looked to Radek for help. Radek met my gaze with a serious look. "Miss Fia, there is a belief that's been passed down for generations among my people. I'd like to talk to you about it. Would you be willing to listen?"

"Huh? Uh, yeah! Sure, of course." Saying *no* really wasn't an option.

"My people believe that the souls of those who possess an especially strong will can be reborn. That we can meet these people again in a new life. That Blue Knight you're so interested in was once the Great Saint's personal knight, and it is recorded in our history that the words you just said about the dolphins and the jellyfish were once spoken by the Great Saint as well. In short...I am certain that *you* are the bearer of the Great Saint's soul. You are the reincarnation of Her Holiness."

I was speechless. He'd just guessed my greatest secret! "Uhhhh..."

Radek gave me a worried look as I trailed off uncertainly. "Are you well? I understand that this is all very sudden for you, and it's understandably hard to believe, but my people truly believe souls with strong wills and a sense of duty are reborn. You could think of this as our wish, perhaps. We owe a great debt to the Great Saint and swore to repay it one day...but were never able to."

He looked sadly at the red flower in my hand before continuing. "The Great Saint promised that she would return here one day, and we've waited ever since. You may think you're not her reincarnation—you may think our ideas strange—but I implore you, as the representative of my people, to at least listen to us and try to understand why we feel this way."

I opened my mouth to speak, but no words followed. What could I say?

"Your actions are too similar to hers to be a mere coincidence. Your interest in the Blue Knight, the personal knight of the Great Saint, is surely a sign that you are her long-awaited reincarnation. Even if we are wrong, please listen to our long-held beliefs. We have waited for so long, you see."

"Uhhh..." My heart throbbed in my chest, and my mind raced.

So, it hasn't been completely revealed that I was the Great Saint in my past life, right? They just believe in reincarnation! It's a religious thing. They think I'm the Great Saint's reincarnation...and they're right! Agh, how did they even figure it out?!

As I screamed internally, Kurtis spoke up, hesitation clear in his voice. "I understand where you're coming from, considering Fia's red hair and her other similarities to the Great Saint, but Fia isn't even a saint."

"I'm aware that she's a knight, but if she's been reincarnated, her body would of course be different. Perhaps her powers didn't transfer over from her previous life. We believe in the reincarnation of the soul, but we've never actually seen anyone else reincarnated before. There is still much to be learned."

"I...see." Kurtis looked unconvinced, probably seeing it as a misunderstanding on the townspeople's part. Still, he couldn't just trample over their feelings, so he continued on as if he agreed. "Now that you mention it, Fia does have both red hair and golden eyes. Yes, I see it now. I'm sure part of her soul was unconsciously drawn to the Blue Knight."

"Wh—C-Captain Kurtis?!" Betrayal!

"We can use this, Fia," he whispered. "If they believe you're the Great Saint's reincarnation, they'll accept you—a knight—with open arms. From there, perhaps they'll accept the rest of us knights as well. This could be our chance to help the Sutherland family and their people to reconcile."

"Ngh..." I glared sharply at him, but he responded by ducking his head and giving me the puppy-dog eyes. *Hnnnngh, those eyes are cheating! But I do want to help Cyril...*

I looked back to Radek and made a face as if I'd just had an epiphany. "Oh, you know what? I think you might be right! Yep, yep! I have a feeling Canopus was my personal knight!"

"You even know Lord Canopus's name?!" someone exclaimed. "You really are the Great Saint! Everyone, she's the real deal!"

The color drained from my face as everyone began to chatter.

Oh. Well, I've sure done it now. I should've been more careful. If I'd really thought about it for even a second, it would've been obvious that Canopus's name was a no go.

Despite my low spirits, Kurtis looked at me with a joyful, thankful smile.

The people celebrated, chanting, "It's the Great Saint!" over and over. I felt my face go stiff.

Wh-what do I do? Was this going to lead to another scolding from Cyril? Maybe if I was lucky, he might actually praise me instead...?

The main event, the dance performance, was completely halted after the first dance. The citizens kept up their fervent chant, "The Great Saint is here! The Great Saint is here!" Things were clearly abnormal, and a report was immediately made to the knight in charge—Cyril. He came as quickly as he could.

Ah, yes, yes. Such a wonderful display of competency. A real boss checks what's wrong with their own eyes.

Cyril ran in just as the chaos reached its peak. His speed was honestly impressive.

Still, wouldn't it have been better to arrive when things had cooled down a bit, for your sake and mine? I thought. The way I see it, he was so competent that he circled back around to incompetent!

The moment he spotted me at the center of all the pandemonium, his face took on the visage of a demon...just like I'd worried.

Eeeeeeeek! He's mad! He's super, super mad! I hid behind Kurtis's back, knowing full well that it was futile.

Without a moment's hesitation, but with a restrained fury in his gait, Cyril walked straight for us. "Chief Radek, Kurtis, what in the world is going on?"

Cyril scanned the area around him, taking in all the chanting townspeople before his gaze came to rest on me, staring daggers.

"Oh, Your Grace!" Radek bowed his head deeply to Cyril. "Thank you for all your help with the festival."

"Not at all, Chief Radek. I should be thanking you for allowing me to host it every year." Cyril made a face like the wind had been taken out of his sails—Radek had obviously dodged his question, after all—but couldn't defy his need to remain courteous.

That was when Radek, as though intentionally aiming to catch Cyril off guard, dropped the bomb. "Incidentally, Your Grace, we've found out that your knight here, Fia, is the reincarnation of Her Holiness the Great Saint."

"I'm...sorry?" Cyril replied. His perfect public relations smile froze on his face.

"Our people believe in the reincarnation of the soul and have been awaiting the Great Saint's return for three hundred years. Fia herself lacks saintly powers and she's rather bewildered by the idea, but she has said things that prove a part of the Great Saint's memory has been passed on to her."

"Yes, I...see." With the same unnatural smile plastered on, Cyril put a finger to his chin.

Ahh, there it is! That's the Cyril in a Bad Mood move!

My flight response took over. I began to creep away backward.

"If at all possible, might we keep Fia here for a while?" Radek asked.

"That's not something I can decide myself," he said. "Fia!"

"Y-yes, Captain!" I cut out the creeping and dashed out from behind Kurtis's back.

Cyril welcomed me with a wide, terrifying smile that was ill fit for the situation. "Now then, would you mind telling me what this is all about? You're the Great Saint's reincarnation, are you? That's certainly news to me."

"Th-the dance! Dolphins! I told them how the dance looked like dolphins, and that's how they confirmed I was the Great Saint!" There, nice and simple.

He furrowed his brow thoughtfully. "Forgive me, I...don't understand how that explains anything."

"Huh? I'm saying that if I'd just said their dance looked like that of a jellyfish, none of this would be happening!" I tried making my explanation even simpler, but he only furrowed his brows even harder.

He turned to Kurtis, giving up on understanding me. "What's your explanation?"

"Yes. Well. The people of this land believe in reincarnation and have particularly longed for the reincarnation of the Great Saint. Some of the comments Fia made while watching the dance were similar to those of the Great Saint, which, alongside the fact that Fia showed interest in the Blue Knight—the Great Saint's own personal knight—led the people to conclude that she was the reincarnation of the Great Saint herself." Kurtis gave an explanation so smooth you'd think it rehearsed.

Something about Kurtis's explanation made Cyril nod with

understanding, despite my simple and easy-to-understand explanations leaving him stumped. "I see."

Kurtis nonchalantly walked up to Cyril and whispered in his ear. "Captain Cyril, while I understand such a thing might go against your beliefs, I think accepting the people's notion of Fia being the Great Saint's reincarnation is the best course of action for now. Fia and I both believe they are mistaken, of course, but we can make use of the fact that they have been waiting for the Great Saint's reincarnation for three hundred years to pay back some debt. This could be the shock to the system you've been looking for!"

Cyril flashed a look of extreme displeasure, but ultimately, he nodded. He glanced at me, and I vigorously nodded my head up and down (the universal sign for agreement). Upon confirming it with a look, he looked back to Radek. "Chief Radek, I find it hard to so quickly believe that Fia is the Great Saint's reincarnation, but I have no objections to letting you all try to confirm such."

"Oh, thank you, Lord Sutherland! We've waited so long for an opportunity to repay the Great Saint!" Overjoyed, Radek clasped Cyril's hands with his own and bowed deeply.

Initially, I'd planned to pig out on food after watching the dances and to use the spending money I'd received from Desmond. That plan never came to fruition, though. Instead Cyril, still smiling radiantly, dragged me back to the mansion against my will. Kurtis, following behind, smiled awkwardly at me as though to say the matter was out of his hands.

"So? What's the meaning of all this?" Cyril brought us to his office and looked the both of us over. Unlike last night, he fully closed the door so that nobody would overhear.

With a troubled face, Kurtis replied, "My earlier explanation was everything I know. I wasn't there to hear it directly, but—from what I gather—the people concluded that Fia was the Great Saint's reincarnation from only a brief exchange." Kurtis glanced over to me for confirmation, and I vigorously nodded my head in agreement.

Mhm, that's right, Captain Kurtis! Everything I said was completely normal, they all just misunderstood on their own accord!

"In other words," Kurtis continued, "the people's longing for the reincarnation of the Great Saint was so strong that they were willing to ignore reality somewhat and treat a person with superficial similarities as her true reincarnation. I imagine they chose Fia because of her red hair. It rubs me as an odd choice—Fia isn't even a saint—but I suppose that's just how desperate they were."

"I...see," Cyril replied. "The people of Sutherland are extremely devout worshippers of the Great Saint. Even though my mother treated them so terribly, they accepted her because she was a red-haired saint...and then came to reject her when she had the Great Saint's Tree cut down. Their values always come back to the Great Saint, don't they?"

Kurtis nodded. "There are many places other than Sutherland that worship the Great Saint. Across many battles, she saved countless knights and citizens, the descendants of whom worshipped her. That being said, there aren't many places that have maintained that worship for the past three centuries the way that Sutherland has...but perhaps that's because she personally visited here. It may have made them feel a more personal connection."

"It may," said Cyril. He walked toward a crammed bookshelf against the wall, stopped in front of some particularly old-looking books, and traced his finger down one of their spines. "I've looked into things, but I cannot find any official records of the Great Saint ever visiting Sutherland. I don't doubt she visited, with there being anniversary festivals, but she couldn't have come for any important business if it was unofficial."

"The people mentioned earlier that Sutherland's lord at the time, the Blue Knight, was the Great Saint's personal knight. Perhaps that's why she visited?" Kurtis suggested. "Whatever the reason may be, it's a well-known fact that the Great Saint did a lot for people everywhere. I can understand the gratitude of the Sutherlanders based on that alone."

I nodded to myself as I watched them talk.

Yep, yep, that was an unofficial visit. I forced my way here on impulse.

"—But regardless, Captain Cyril, I think we should make use of this opportunity. Fia isn't the kind to offend anyone, so I see no problem letting the people believe she is the Great Saint's reincarnation. If things go well, the people might warm up to the knights and to you, returning things to how they used to be around here."

"You mean back before my parents came to govern? Yes, perhaps. I do have a responsibility to undo what my parents caused," Cyril said, speaking from the heart.

I nodded along again. *I believe in you, Captain Cyril. You have both maturity and a willingness to admit mistakes, which are qualities required of a lord. If anyone can improve relations, it's you! You can do it!*

"Are you okay with this, Fia?" asked Cyril, his voice heavy with worry. "It isn't exactly what you signed up for."

I flashed a wide grin. "No problem at all! Pretending to be the Great Saint's reincarnation? Sounds like a piece of cake!" *Gonna be easy enough to pretend that I am who I am, after all! Heh heh heh!*

"Still...I know I'm already asking a lot of you, but please try to show some moderation. The Great Saint is a revered figure. Don't forget that."

"Ho ho ho! Don't worry 'bout a thing, Captain Cyril!" I said, brimming with confidence.

For some reason, the two of them each let out a real mammoth of a sigh.

I've been entrusted with an important duty: assuming the role of the beautiful, noble, and tender-hearted Great Saint. Honestly, they really couldn't have chosen a better person for the role! I mean, I *am* the Great Saint in question, you know?

I was granted the revered title of Great Saint three hundred years ago. There was no telling how much history was passed down or prettied up, all these centuries later. There'd always been a chance that the facts were so twisted that people would think I was a nobody.

Still, the people of this land remained fervent worshippers of the Great Saint. Surely *they* wouldn't think anything negative about me.

But...then again, the saints themselves have become pretty twisted, and nobody seems to have voiced any objection to the changes. What if something weird about me *had* passed down, and nobody even thought twice about it in this day and age because everything has changed so much?

N-no, no, never! That would be impossible! I always acted sensibly! I was totally upstanding all my life—and in this life, for that matter. My personal knight Canopus, and even the royal guards, were always strict with teaching me. No way anybody would get the wrong idea about me after all these years.

Suddenly self-conscious, I straightened my back and coolly looked into the mirror. *Oh? Who's that serious badass looking back at me? I actually look pretty tough!*

As I admired my reflection, I heard a voice from behind me.

"Fia...I don't know what kind of image you have of the Great Saint, but perhaps a gentler expression would suit you for this?" said Cyril hesitantly. I could see him in the reflection in the mirror. "Or are you playing around and pretending to be a Great Saint who's angry at the world? One full of indignation who might—oh, I don't know, do something like proclaim 'The saints have become twisted,' to borrow your own words."

"I am doing no such thing, Captain Cyril! I'm just trying to look tough and serious. I'm not angry in the slightest. Anyway, what do you think? Don't I just exude dignity and nobility?"

"I'm...rather ignorant of such things and couldn't possibly judge. Perhaps Kurtis could give you a proper answer?" Cyril said, smoothly passing the question to the knight beside him.

"Wh-what?!" Kurtis exclaimed. "But, Captain Cyril! There's no way someone as great as you couldn't answer something that I could! Um, well, uh...you look like a...grumpy...knight?"

"What a shallow take!" I exclaimed. "You lack the imagination to read between the lines of my expression! And I'm not grumpy at all! I'm just stiffening my face to look serious!"

Cyril and Kurtis simply smiled awkwardly in reply.

Ah, these two are hopeless. They don't have the sensitivity needed to sense the dignity I'm exuding!

I turned my back to the pair and politely excused myself from Cyril's office. I returned to my assigned room and took out a travel bag and a light-blue dress—I couldn't wear the knight uniform while pretending to be the Great Saint, after all. I put the dress on. It was a little wrinkled, but not bad enough to be a problem. The skirt came down to my knees, so I could wear my knight's boots without any fashion-clashing. I spun once to check how the dress fluttered, then left my room, satisfied.

I passed by Cyril's office and could vaguely make out two people talking inside, presumably Cyril and Kurtis. I didn't want to bother them, so I informed the mansion's butler that I was leaving for town and to please tell Captain Cyril, if he looked for me later.

I *definitely* wasn't avoiding the two captains because I didn't want them to tag along and make my excursion all awkward or anything. Perish the thought.

Finally, I can make use of Captain Desmond's spending money, I pondered as I walked outside. Soon enough, some townspeople saw me and came running over, smiling happily as they called to me.

"Welcome back, Your Holiness!"

"We've been waiting for you, Your Holiness!"

"I'm so happy you've returned, Your Holiness!"

It wasn't that long ago the chief said I might be the reincarnation of the Great Saint, but word had spread like wildfire. I was a bit overwhelmed, but I liked seeing the townspeople with smiles instead of wary looks.

I found myself smiling back and replied, albeit a bit awkwardly. "Thank you for the welcome, but it's not certain I'm the Great Saint yet. I don't have any saint powers or any memories of the time I was the Great Saint."

The job wasn't to pretend to be the Great Saint, after all. I had to pretend that I *might* be the Great Saint, so I had to leave some room for doubt. I didn't exactly consult with anyone about this part of the plan, but I wanted things to be a little ambiguous when I eventually left Sutherland. That way, I didn't have to disappoint the townspeople completely by making them "realize" I *wasn't* the Great Saint.

At any rate, everyone thought I didn't have any saint powers, so there probably wouldn't be any big problems even if I did go all out with my performance. The townspeople would just be happy to repay what they felt they owed the Great Saint. Cyril and Kurtis didn't believe that I was the Great Saint's reincarnation, so I couldn't see any reason why it wouldn't all just blow over once we left Sutherland. As for demons, they don't interact with humans much. Even if there was a bit of commotion here in Sutherland, it probably wouldn't spread so far that demons caught wind of it, or of me. Besides, the demon who killed me in my past life said he would find and kill me again if I were reborn as a saint, but...it'd be fine as long as nobody ever found out about my saint powers, right?

"Right?" I muttered, double-checking my logic.

The townspeople beamed at me.

"Ha ha! You needn't overthink it. I, at the very least, believe you are the Great Saint!"

"Me too! Oh, and your hair is just so beautiful! It really is the color of dawn, like everyone says! Look how it shines in the sunlight..."

"Huh? R-really? Thank you," I stammered with a smile.

An elderly woman wrapped her trembling hand around mine. "Welcome back, Your Holiness. Thank you for returning at such a time."

"Hm? Such a time?" I repeated, tilting my head.

Teary-eyed, the elderly woman swallowed. "No...never mind."

Was she referring to the annual festival that had been going for three hundred years?

I held her hand tightly. "Sutherland is a beautiful place. The sea, the forest, the town, everything here is beautiful. I'm glad I could visit."

The elderly woman gripped my hand. "We're honored to receive you," she said and bowed deeply before leaving.

I was watching her go, a bit confused, when a group of children appeared running toward me from the same direction. They were the same children that we'd saved from the Basilisk the other day.

"Your Holiness!" they yelled and lined up to hug me, one after the other.

"Ha ha! Why, hello! You all haven't gone to the forest again, have you?" I asked, lifting one of the children into my arms.

The child shook their head. "We won't do anything dangerous anymore! The Great Saint saved our lives, so we gotta be extra sure to treasure them!"

"Well, aren't you a bunch of good boys and girls?" I said, letting the child down. The other children, still hugging my legs, smiled up at me.

"I knew you were the real Great Saint all along, ever since I saw you on the beach!"

"Me too, me too! Because your hair's so red! Mommy said the Great Saint has hair the color of, um...of early in the mornin'! So I knew it!"

Oh...right. It was mainly my hair that made people think I was the Great Saint. Not that they were wrong, of course. This world was just a little too simple sometimes.

I giggled and began walking hand in hand with the children. "All right, let's go eat something together so you all can grow big and strong! What's good around here?"

"That shop is the best! They grill fruits and sprinkle sugar on top! They have lots of fruits to choose from, so you can choose your favorite!" The children pointed to a store with red, yellow, and green fruits on display.

"Wow, you guys are right, that does look good!" I chose a dark-red fruit that caught my eye. Then I remembered just how much spending money Desmond had given me and decided to treat the children. "You all choose something too. Food tastes better when you eat together, don't you think?"

The children happily chose their fruit, selecting from colorful and appetizing, red, yellow, green, and even orange fruits. After the children made their selections, I asked the shopkeeper how much it would cost.

"Huh? N-no, you needn't pay a thing! I wouldn't dare take money from the Great Saint!" the shopkeeper cried, waving his hands as if the very idea was wildly absurd.

But I couldn't allow myself not to pay. "It's not set in stone that I'm the Great Saint's reincarnation, though. Please, I insist."

"No, no, no! If I were to do that, my family would make me sleep on the streets!"

"That can't be true... If I take this for free, I'd basically be swindling you by using the Great Saint's name! My captain would make *me* sleep out on the streets!" Cyril was such an honest man—I truly wouldn't put it past him.

Oddly enough, however, the townspeople around me began to take the shopkeeper's side.

"It's true, Your Holiness. The shopkeeper's wife is terrifying!"

"The shopkeeper married into his wife's family! If she wanted to, she could drive *him* out of the house! Please, don't pay! For his sake!"

"Whaaaaaat?!"

In the end, I relented to the will of the crowd and didn't pay, leaving the shop without getting a chance to use any of Desmond's spending money. Still, the children looked happy with their fruit. I guess all's well that ends well?

Feeling a bit conflicted, I bit into my sugary treat. My eyes shot open the instant I tasted the sweet, tangy flavor. "Mmm, this is good! Delicious, even!"

The children and I talked about how yummy the sugared fruits were as we walked until they pointed out a shop with a yellow signboard out front.

"Your Holiness, look! That's the amber sweets shop!"

"The shopkeeper is really, really good at making amber sweets! He can make them into any shape!"

"Oh?" I said, wondering what amber sweets were. Were they just sweets that were amber colored? I'd only attended small festivals as a child, and these were the kind of sweets they only carried at specialty shops, so this was my first time seeing them.

We walked into the store and were greeted by an enthusiastic shopkeeper. "Your Holiness! Please, allow me to create you!"

I tilted my head at him. *Huh? What the heck does that mean?*

The shopkeeper stood up straight and began pouring pots of liquified sugar onto an iron plate, as if making a picture from the sugary goop. They made lines of different thickness by deftly controlling how much they poured out of the pots, creating a compelling picture right before my eyes.

They eventually stopped, gave a satisfied nod, and put a stick on the finished product. The amber candy soon hardened, and the shopkeeper gave it to me with a proud look on their face. "I've finished, Your Holiness! I made it as big as possible, so I hope you'll eat as much of my work as you can!"

I silently appraised the amber candy, holding it by the stick that served as its handle. It was well done. In just a short amount of time, the shopkeeper had made an impressive candy picture of the Great Saint. But...did they really have to make it so big? The picture was wonderful, depicting the Great Saint standing tall in her dress, but my figure looked a little, uh...round.

"Sure, I sometimes pig out till my tummy sticks out, but this is a little much..." I grumbled.

"I'm sorry? Did you say something, Your Holiness?"

I flashed a smile. "I-I said *thank you so much, this is wonderful!*" A mature adult like myself can't let something trivial like this get to me, especially when I was pretending to be the benevolent Great Saint.

But man, I thought as the kids and I left the amber candy store behind, *pretending to be the Great Saint is tough!*

The children and I went on to visit many other shops, but I never got a chance to spend any money at them. Every time I insisted that I should pay, and every time the local townspeople would insist back that I shouldn't, out of consideration for the shopkeepers. Many times did I taste defeat—and snacks—at the hands of the townspeople.

The kids and I stuffed ourselves until we were full, then they thanked me and returned home. They rubbed their eyes as they went, clearly ready for nap time.

With some luck, I managed to slip away from the throngs of townspeople and went down an alley in search of another new store. The townspeople I passed on the way there eyed my red hair with curiosity but quickly averted their eyes without saying anything. It appeared rumors of me being the Great Saint's reincarnation hadn't spread everywhere quite yet. Maybe now I'd have a proper chance to spend some money. I'd just begun to look around when I made eye contact with a man in his thirties.

The man gasped. Then he drew near and pointed farther down the alley. "You can find something nice to eat down there."

I looked down the alley, but there didn't seem to be anything resembling a store around. Cyril had warned me not to follow strangers promising food, though, so I grew wary. I shook my head. "Thank you very much, but I'm actually looking to rest a bit right now."

The man snatched my arm impatiently. "S-somebody's sick! They need help!"

What?! Someone's sick?! That changes everything!

I ran through the alley together with the man and bounded around the corner to find a group of men waiting. Puzzlingly, they all appeared to be in fine health.

But you can't always tell from a glance, right? Just then, a hand reached out and covered my mouth. I looked down, shocked—a man was pressing a cloth against my mouth.

A second passed. Another second. Nothing happened. A third second went by...

"Wh-why isn't she losing consciousness?!" exclaimed the man holding the cloth to my mouth. He looked around at the other men. "The paralysis effect on this should be instant!" He snarled.

Always helps to be a saint, I thought. Weak status ailments just rolled right off me.

I pushed the hand from my mouth and looked each of the five men squarely in the face. "So, where is this sick person? Or has there been a mistake? If you're all healthy, may I please continue my shopping?"

"Uh, no, there is a sick person, but, um..."

"Well..."

The men seemed to hesitate for some reason.

I tilted my head. "I assume you guys were trying to knock me unconscious and bring me to wherever this sick person is, right? I appreciate it, but I can walk there by myself. You could just show me the way like normal. Yes, I'm light as a feather, so I can understand why you'd consider carrying me, but I really can just walk myself."

There I was, slipping a mention of my weight in. Man, the

incident with the amber candy must have still been dragging me down.

One of the men spoke up. "Th-that's right, but...h-how can you be so kind? We just tried to abduct you. Why aren't you running away?"

That confirmed my suspicions: These guys hadn't heard the rumors that I was the Great Saint's reincarnation. If they did know, they'd be treating me with way more respect, like the townspeople from earlier. Plus, they would've also heard that I didn't have any saint powers and so they wouldn't have tried their whole heal-the-sick ruse. Their actions were probably impulsive, betting that someone with my hair color *might* have saint powers. Still, it was pretty rash. Maybe they were really, *really* at their wit's end?

"Well, if someone's sick," I said, "I want to do what I can to help. Buuuut then again, maybe you guys were trying to kidnap me for nefarious reasons?" I eyed the swords on their hips. You didn't often see weapons that nice on people who weren't knights.

The men started babbling protests. "P-perish the thought! We wouldn't—we'd never—I mean— never!" The men denied, frantically waving their hands. They all turned to one particular man in their group for help.

With some hesitation, the man stepped forward before me and bowed his head. "Please, forgive our violent actions earlier. I am Ariel, grandson of the chief. The sick person in question is my daughter. I would be grateful to have your help."

The man who called himself Ariel appeared to be in his mid-twenties. He had the dark-brown skin and dark-blue hair characteristic of the former islander peoples, and he nervously scratched his chin with a bony finger.

Is he nervous because he feels guilty about something? "Nice to meet you. I am Fia Ruud. I will hold no grudge, but you should really try just explaining yourself next time."

The five men bowed apologetically. They couldn't be bad people if they were this polite, right?

I stared them down. "I don't particularly mind—because I can get away with my saint powers and all—but for any other person, as soon as you tried to cover their mouth, they'd be too scared to go along with you. Keep that in mind for next time."

"Then we're lucky that we met you," one of the men said nervously.

The men led me to a cave along the beach. The entrance was small, but it widened the further we proceeded inside. At the back, the area opened into a wide cavern.

Straining my eyes, I saw about half of the space was filled by around fifty people, all sleeping. Even from a distance, I could tell they were all sick, and their breathing labored. I drew closer. Their limply stretched out limbs had a distinct yellow pattern along them.

"Oh...this is..." I recognized the symptoms: yellow patterns along the arms and legs, labored breathing, and fever. This was...

Ariel, who'd been silently waiting by my side all worried, suddenly looked toward the entrance of the cavern and squinted. "Who's there?!"

Surprised, I looked back to see a dark figure about fifteen meters away near the entrance. It was hard to make out who it was in the darkness, but the faint torchlight gleamed across what appeared to be the collar of a knight uniform gleam. I bent forward, trying to get a better look, when the dark figure slowly stepped out of the shadows. I couldn't quite make out their face yet, but I recognized the light-blue hair that came down to their shoulders.

"Captain Kurtis?!" I shouted. *Huh? Wh-what is he doing here? Did he see me with Ariel and the rest and follow along, worried?*

Eyes wide, I watched him walk forward and unsheathe his sword.

"Huh? C-Captain Kurtis, calm down! Please, sheathe your sword!" I pleaded, but he paid me no mind and continued forward with forceful steps. I stared in shock. He normally looked so kind, but now he was downright threatening.

He seemed to make his mind up about something and looked around a bit impatiently. Then it hit me: *That's right, Captain Kurtis is in charge of this area! Of course, he'd feel something's wrong if people were skulking about right under his nose!*

I was about to reassure him nothing bad was happening, but before I could, a group of people who'd heard Ariel shouting gathered around. The five who guided me were there, as well as some others who kept watch around the cave. They drew near Kurtis and put their hands on their sword hilts.

"What can one knight do?!" One of them sneered. "We all have years of experience fighting as a vigilante group!" He was clearly looking for a fight.

"Huh? W-wait, what about the Sutherland vow of pacifism?!"

But my words fell on empty ears. Everyone was focusing on Kurtis. *Th-this is bad!*

The men were so focused on protecting the sick people behind them, they'd completely forgotten about their vow.

I tried running to Kurtis, but only got a few steps before Ariel grabbed my arm. Despite my training with the brigade, I found I couldn't break away. Perhaps men of the sea were just that much more powerful.

"Ariel, let me go!" I demanded, glaring. I couldn't let Kurtis and the men start fighting. Someone was sure to get hurt that way.

As I tried to free myself from Ariel's grip, several men charged at Kurtis. They surrounded him and wordlessly unsheathed their swords. Kurtis readied his blade. A tense silence fell.

The first to break the silence was the man positioned behind Kurtis. He rushed in and swung his sword down from above. Kurtis spun around and smoothly parried the blade to his side, but the men positioned to his immediate left and right didn't miss the opportunity—they both thrust their swords as one.

Ka-kling! The ring of clashing steel echoed across the cave. Aiming at his blind spots, sword after sword came after Kurtis, thrusting and slicing from all directions. Fighting alone against multiple adversaries was difficult. Kurtis was a captain, but he lacked the overwhelming strength the other captains had. Eventually, he took the brunt of one of the countless strikes right in the arm. Blood splashed.

"Captain Kurtis!" I yelled, finally shaking off Ariel's grip and running to Kurtis.

But the attacks didn't stop. Kurtis tried his best to avoid the onslaught, but a single sword thrust found its mark and impaled him through his back. His shoulder and neck were hacked up too. Fresh blood sprayed into the air.

"Stop it! Stop it!"

By the time I reached him, his body had been pierced by several more sword strikes. Blood pooled on the cave floor beneath him. The life was beginning to fade from his eyes.

"Captain Kurtis, pull yourself together!" I shrieked. He seemed to react somewhat and propped himself up by thrusting his sword into the ground...but his hold on consciousness was dim, and his eyes unfocused.

I could only catch pieces of his muttering. "Get...back... Lady...se...fi...a..." Then his body gave out, and he collapsed.

"C-Captain Kurtis!" My scream echoed through the cavern, mingling with the heavy sound of his body thudding against the earth.

More blood seeped from his body, staining the ground red.

I moved a hand over to his pale face, his closed eyes. "Captain Kurtis! Please, wake up!"

My voice echoed throughout the cave, but there was no response.

A Tale of the Secret Saint

Canopus, Personal Knight

(THREE HUNDRED YEARS AGO)

I KNOW THE GREATEST SIN of my life. I know it all too well.

What years remain to me, I have spent in regret, reliving the moment I failed her on and on, through the long, relentless days. But my regrets—my laments, my begging, my prayers—fall on empty ears. The past will not change.

It takes but a moment to lose something precious. What is gone can never return.

Her dawn-red hair, her smile full of tenderness, her gentle voice—they are gone forever.

What meaning does my life hold now?

I was amidst a dream, and I was serving her once again. It was another world, a different world, and I knew it must be a dream—or perhaps I had died? Yes, perhaps I had departed to a place where I could at last know peace.

She was as I remembered her: red hair, golden eyes, untroubled smile. Although I had no right to weep, tears fell from my eyes the moment I saw her.

This...this was the sight I had failed to protect. This was the woefully beautiful view that now lay beyond my reach.

Once again, as I had done countless times over on the long days without her, I made my vow to her.

"If I could be reborn and serve you again, I would surely protect you from everyone and everything in this world. This time, I would."

Hearing this, the girl in my dream smiled happily.

"...opus! Canopus!"

I heard my name and woke up with a start. Sitting up, I could feel that my nightwear was drenched in sweat. My heart was pounding.

"Whoa, are you crying or something?"

Surprised, I touched below my eyes. I was shocked to find my fingers brushing tears. How many years had it been since I last cried?

"I...must've been dreaming. Though I cannot recall what..." I stood up and faced the knight I was rooming with. It was true—I could not recall a thing.

"Ha ha! Take it as a hint, eh?" The knight was two years my senior and fond of joking. "Your future self, maybe. Telling you that her Highness the Second Princess might just turn you away. Leave you crying in your sleep!"

Putting on my knight uniform, I shrugged. "At least I won't be the only one," I said calmly. "More than a hundred knights will be rejected today."

"Right, right. And look at you! One of the hundred lucky enough to even *get* a rejection!"

We cracked jokes back and forth as we left the room, making for the canteen.

Today, the second princess was choosing her personal knight. I was one of only one hundred-something chosen as a candidate. I was sure my chances of being chosen were slim, but perhaps fate had something else in store.

My name is Canopus Blazej, a knight of the Náv Kingdom. My ancestry traces back to an island south of the continent. I lived in Sutherland amongst my own people until I turned thirteen, and then I ventured forth to the royal capital in hopes of becoming a knight.

Not many of my people lived in the royal capital, and I suffered some discrimination for my dark-brown skin and webbed hands. The bigotry rankled me at first—I spoke back—but in time I became indifferent to it. Talking back changed nothing, after all.

As luck would have it, my sword skills and good etiquette received notice, and I was made a knight the same year I set out for the royal capital. Still, I was a commoner and of the former islander peoples; no matter how hard I worked, I would never rise above a rank-and-file knight.

My luck changed one day, when I was seventeen. I, along with a number of other knights, had gathered in the castle's great hall. Today, the second princess would be choosing her personal knight from over one hundred candidates—or at least, that was how things appeared on the surface. In reality, I was sure that her personal knight was already pre-selected. They had to be. After all, a guard for the second princess must be willing to die for her. Surely they had researched all possible candidates already and come to a conclusion.

Besides, only those from high-ranking noble families were truly in the running. Though there were many talented and loyal people like myself from the lower class, society did not see us as equals. Not yet, anyway.

I passed time with such ponderings when, finally, the grand door ahead of us opened and a crowd of people came in. Everyone present lowered their heads. When we finally raised our heads again, an adorable little princess stood before us. She was the second princess, and she shared the same deep-crimson hair as the first princess—proof that she was a powerful saint.

She stood a few steps up on a platform, and I supposed now that she would announce her choice. Instead, to everybody's surprise, she jumped off and began walking toward us. She smiled, then curtsied in a rather adorable fashion. "It is nice to meet you all," she said. "I am Serafina, the second princess. Today, I shall choose one of you to be my personal knight."

Serafina, the second princess, giggled as she strode before us, though her legs were not yet long, and her stride was sweet and youthful. *What an utterly adorable walk,* I thought...and then, quite suddenly, she stopped right in front of me.

Her eyes were bright with surprise. "You're strong..." she said. "What's your name?"

"Canopus Blazej, Your Highness." Shocked as I was to be addressed, I managed to remain calm.

The princess smiled happily back at me. "Canopus, will you be my personal knight?"

I froze on the spot, as did the other knights present and the high-ranking officials waiting to the side. Soon after, however, the officials came running over to the princess.

"Y-Your Highness, please—this isn't your personal knight," an official said. "You have a name already, remember? Go on! Say it, won't you?"

"Father said I can choose who I want."

"P-p-perhaps, yes. The name we've given you is of course a mere suggestion, but every member of royalty before you has heeded our wisdom in this matter. I implore you to do so as well."

"Y-yes!" another advisor appealed to her. "And behold the hair, the skin—this man is one of those islanders, is he not? He lacks the appropriate background to be your knight, Your Highness."

The officials desperately tried to sway the princess's mind, but she ignored them all. "Thank you for the advice," she said, still smiling. "But I choose Canopus. What say you, Canopus? Will you be my personal knight?"

She repeated herself, looking at me with eyes full of expectation. I glanced at the officials to her side to see them shaking their

heads with fierce intensity, but there was no way I could do what they were asking of me. I came to the capital with hopes of becoming the princess's knight. To refuse her offer at this point? Lunacy.

I took a knee and performed the knight salute. "I, Canopus Blazej, pledge to serve Your Highness Second Princess Serafina Náv with all my being. Glory and blessings be to Her Highness."

After saying that, I lowered my head and completed my pledge of loyalty by kissing the hem of her dress. With that, she smiled and turned around to face the vice-commander of the knight brigade—also a close aide of the princess—as he approached with his sword.

"To guard the royal family," said the vice-commander, "you must be willing to give up your life at any moment. I do hope you won't place your life before that of Her Highness." He handed me the sword and continued. "Receive this blade and be officially dubbed the personal knight of Her Highness the Second Princess Serafina."

The sword weighed heavily in my hands. From the vice-commander's near glare, I could feel just how much he cared for the second princess. A profound duty had been bestowed upon me.

I reflected on what had transpired and thanked the princess for the opportunity from the bottom of my heart. Perhaps her youth had simply left her unaware of the rules of the world, but she had forgone convention by choosing me, a man with no standing, over the high-ranking noble who was surely meant to be her personal knight.

The future I envisioned only moments earlier—a future of equity and balance—had seemed impossible, but this young princess made it a reality before my very eyes. With mere words, the noble princess had shaped the world...and now I had the privilege of serving her.

I heaved a great breath, rendered speechless. I swore to myself I would serve the princess with whole-hearted devotion.

This was the miracle. This was the day I was selected as the personal knight of a member of the royal family.

Ten years of serving Serafina as her personal knight passed, and she turned sixteen. Before I knew it, she had become a healthy young woman.

At the age of fifteen, she was recognized for her merits and ability, and became the first in our kingdom to bear the title of Great Saint. Unfortunately, this made her life much busier than it had been before. Every moment of Serafina's existence, from dawn to sunset, was strictly managed. She joined monster extermination expeditions for days on end. She was made to visit over ten relief centers in a single day. And yet, despite her hectic schedule, she never once complained.

Her schedule was planned out a year in advance too. As such, it was near impossible for her to handle emergency requests, even when they were requested by those of great influence.

One day, an envoy delivered news to me of my homeland. The yellow-speckle fever had spread rapidly in Sutherland, and they were requesting I send the Great Saint to visit. This yellow-speckle fever was a rather common disease, and nearly all citizens got it as a child. It induced a light fever and caused yellow-colored speckles to appear across the skin of the arms and legs. Adults rarely caught it, but those adults who did suffered symptoms far milder than the children.

Or at least, that was the case for those who weren't former islanders. When *we* contracted the disease, the yellow-colored speckles extended beyond the arms and legs to cover the entire body, and the afflicted was racked with a high fever that muddled their mind. In time, death followed. Our local doctors guessed that the isolation of our island meant our people lacked the protections against yellow-speckle fever that the mainlanders had developed.

It took only about a month for a former islander afflicted with the disease to die. By the time the envoy had left to warn us, about a tenth of the people in Sutherland had contracted the illness. And it spread quickly, like fire...

"The tasks of Her Holiness are determined by the high-ranking officials in a meeting. I, as well as the chief, have requested aid numerous times in the half-year since the disease first sprung up, but we haven't been selected yet. All that is left to us is to wait," I replied, repeating the same words I'd been saying for six months.

"The mainlanders discriminate against our people!" The envoy roared.

"They won't select us no matter how long we wait! Neither the saints in Sutherland nor the powerful saints we've called upon from other locales have bothered to help us cure this plague!

We wait for the guidance of Her Holiness—or is her kingdom telling our people to simply die?!"

The envoy's feelings gnawed at me—why, I had even felt them myself. The fellow was from the same hometown as I. And yet... "I accompany Her Holiness wherever she goes. Every day, she handles matters where lives are on the line. While it's hard to decide who lives and who dies, the high-ranking officials do their best to prioritize those in the most need. All we can do is wait."

A half-truth. Among Serafina's duties, there were ceremonies and other events involving high-ranking nobility that were politically vital, but certainly not matters of life or death. I avoided mentioning them. I also avoided bringing up the fact that Sutherland was terribly far away. If Serafina were to be sent to Sutherland, it would take around three weeks for her to make a round trip. Having accompanied her for quite some time, I knew firsthand how valuable her time was and how unreasonable it was for Sutherland to monopolize so much of it.

But how could I say such a thing to the envoy?

He grabbed my collar. "Have you become the royal family's dog?!" he roared. "How can you talk like this doesn't concern you?! You're Her Holiness's personal knight! Ask her to help us yourself, damn you!"

"I could. Her Holiness, in all her benevolence, would likely lend an ear to my pleas and urge the high-ranking officials to add the matter to her schedule...but that would be wrong. Don't you see? Nobody can be shown undue favoritism by Her Holiness.

And I am merely her personal knight. I would never do anything that is not to her benefit."

"Canopus!" The envoy glared daggers at me. I returned his gaze, saying nothing.

Even if the request were added to Serafina's schedule, it would take over a year to be fulfilled. Given the rapid spread of the disease, it would surely be too late by then. By the time she arrived, only the few tens or hundreds who overcame the disease on their own would remain.

It would be hard to carry on our proud traditions with so few survivors. At this rate, the death of our culture was assured. That being the case, I'd tried to persuade the chief to migrate, for the disease was sure to spread unabated as long as we remained. Quarantining so many infected was difficult. Sending all the infected to the royal capital for treatment from Serafina? Unfeasible. The only option was to abandon Sutherland and split into three groups heading north, east, and west.

But the chief didn't approve of my suggestion. The yellow-speckle fever was prevalent everywhere, he explained, and migrating wouldn't change that. Moreover, our people had already abandoned our ancestral home after the eruption of the volcano on our island. Having to forsake one's home once was already one time too many. Furthermore, scattering our people to the winds meant that we might never be truly whole again.

After listening to the chief's quiet explanation, I couldn't bring myself to argue any more. Miserably, I left the room and saw the envoy off.

"Heya, Canopus—what's up?"

Unfortunately, I bumped into Serafina. I cursed my luck. "Good evening, Lady Serafina. I was just bidding goodbye to an acquaintance. Isn't it rather late in the evening for a walk??"

"Oh, please! You don't need to fuss over me when you're off the clock. Besides, I have these knights accompanying me." She turned with a smile to look at the knights waiting behind her. They wore the red-colored knight uniform of the Great Saint's elite Royal Guard.

"So, what're *you* doing out this late?" she asked with curious eyes. "Secretly meeting with your sweetheart? Then again, it looked like a guy...so was it somebody from Sutherland?"

She must've caught a glimpse of the envoy's dark-brown skin and dark-blue hair as he left. Hoping to end the conversation before she caught on to things, I put on my usual face. "Indeed. I became an earl and was given dominion over Sutherland when you became Great Saint. Ever since then, I've received periodic updates from an envoy, like the one you just saw."

"Ohhh, I see. Heh heh, the people of Sutherland must be over-joyed to have one of their own as their lord! On top of that, you get to be the 'Blue Knight!' A Sutherlander gets to be one of the two knights to represent the white and blue of our flag—isn't that great?"

I frowned and looked down at the knight uniform I wore—it wasn't the red of the Great Saint's Royal Guard but a blue knight uniform.

"While it is an honor," I admitted, "I am a bit conflicted about not wearing the Royal Guard uniform anymore."

The captain of the Royal Guards ordered me to wear the blue knight uniform to show that I was proud to bear the honorable title of Blue Knight. Although, personally, I felt there was far more honor in the red uniforms that declared one's service to Serafina.

She smiled, amused, as if she could read my mind. "Oh, you, I bet you think you'd find more honor in being part of the Royal Guard rather than being the one and only Blue Knight. You truly are devoted. The people of Sutherland are lucky to have a lord like you."

"I am unworthy of such praise."

"Oh yeah, and speaking of blue... I heard the ocean around Sutherland is *unbelievably* blue! I'd love to see it sometime." Her eyes twinkled hopefully. She genuinely looked her age when she was like this.

"I'd love to show you around Sutherland someday as well."

"Then it's a promise, Canopus." She smiled, then walked off toward her room with her Royal Guards following after.

As I feared, the yellow-speckle disease showed no signs of slowing down in Sutherland. Letter after letter arrived, requesting Serafina's assistance. Only two weeks after his previous visit, the envoy came to speak to me again.

"The situation worsens by the minute! We simply cannot wait any longer! I beg you, please send Her Holiness to Sutherland!"

From his bloodshot eyes, clearly visible even in the dark, I could tell he'd sacrificed sleep to ride here as quickly as possible.

"I understand how you feel," I answered. "I also want Her Holiness to help. But Her Holiness is too busy; she cannot afford to be away for three weeks' time. Moreover, no matter what channels we go through, it would take at least a year for her to be dispatched. It'll be too late by then, so...we simply must find another way."

"We've tried every other way there is—we've called on the most esteemed saints from all over the kingdom, but not a single one of them could heal the disease! Perhaps not even Her Holiness can manage such a thing, but she's the only option we have left!" The envoy was frantic with desperation. "The yellow-speckle disease is spreading fast. We'll be wiped out in less than a year at this rate. Please, send Her Holiness! I beg of you!"

The envoy fell to his knees and pleaded. I understood how he felt so much it hurt. Unable to find the words for a reply, I sank into silence.

The envoy was right; our people would be annihilated if nothing changed. He was also right that Serafina was our only hope. But that did not change the fact that she was too important to the kingdom to be sent away for so long. She made unwinnable battles winnable, made incurable injuries and curses curable... There was simply too much that only she could achieve. Taking up three weeks of her time was unimaginable.

I hung my head, seeing no options left, when suddenly a crass voice called out. "Oh, what's this? I was wondering who could be blocking the corridor, and it turns out it's Canopus. So hard to tell with your dark skin, islander! Get out of the way, would you? Or would you rather be executed for daring to block the path of royalty?!"

I spun to face the speaker. The second prince, Capella, walked down the corridor, accompanied by Serafina and a number of other high officials. Surprised by my own inattention, I let out a small groan before quickly grabbing the envoy and moving the two of us to the edge of the corridor.

It was my mistake. I'd gotten so wrapped up in the envoy's hastiness that I started our meeting in the hallway before we even entered my chamber. I kept my head down and prayed that the group would walk past.

Instead, Capella stopped before us. "What is this, a strategy meeting for you ex-islanders? Perhaps you're just trying to figure out what to do after your people are wiped off the map, hmm? Ha! Learn from Canopus's example and lick Serafina's boots, why don't you? That's the way to get a place in the Royal Castle, far away from that diseased backwater of yours."

This was the envoy's first time in the presence of royalty. He trembled, daring not even raise his head. I hesitated for a moment, wondering how to respond, but before I could come up with anything, Serafina spoke.

"Brother, what do you mean by that? How would they be wiped off the map?"

Shocked, I quickly looked up and saw a sickening grin on Capella's face "Oh, you didn't know? There's an epidemic raging across Canopus's territory, Sutherland. Every meeting, we go over a petition he submits requesting that you be dispatched there. Of course, I'm a part of those meetings. Every time, not a single person is in favor of the petition. Your schedule is determined far in advance—you have no room for such piddling requests."

"What kind of disease is it?" she asked.

"Ha ha ha! It's the yellow-speckle fever of all things! A simple disease that even babies in the mainland recover from! Can you believe it? A child's disease kills these former islanders! And it's spreading like wildfire there! A degenerate race like their own is clearly unfit to survive in this world. I say, good riddance."

Serafina quietly listened to her brother's words, then tilted her head, confused. "But the former islanders number tens of thousands, I've heard. If the disease threatens so many people, why haven't I been sent already?"

"Pfft—just how dull are you?! Sutherland is at least ten days away. To go there and back would take three weeks or more. The Royal Capital already has many people needing aid. How are we supposed to send you away for three weeks?!"

Seeing that Serafina was still confused, he continued. "Do I need to spell everything out for you? It would be a different matter if it were mainland citizens, but these are the former islanders we're talking about. They're a lower race—what does it matter if they're wiped out. Not a single person in this castle would support sending you away to aid them. Everyone here is a mainlander, after all."

"Oh...I see. I understand now, thank you very much." She bowed to Capella and clenched her jaw.

The attitude her older brothers took with her always irked me. Serafina didn't receive much of the education that the rest of the royal family enjoyed, instead it was her duty to spend time improving herself as a saint.

Of course, never for a single moment did I believe that Serafina, who held love for all her subjects, would ever treat other ethnic groups differently...which made the prince's mockery even more aggravating to me. Still, Serafina acted as though she didn't mind her brother's words. She simply turned her back to him and faced the envoy. "As you've just heard, this choice is out of my hands. That being said, while I don't know if it'll amount to anything, I'll make sure to request that I be allowed to help. Don't give up hope just yet."

"Th-thank you so very much! We shall eagerly await a visit from Your Holiness!" The envoy clasped his hands above his head in reverent prayer to Serafina.

Her few words gave hope to the envoy. Filled with love and understanding for her people, she always had the right words to make their hearts soar. Nevertheless, I was certain the envoy knew full well that those words were the limit of what she could do for Sutherland—he'd heard the venomous words of the prince, after all. Serafina's heart brimmed with compassion, but compassion alone could not save Sutherland.

Or so I had believed. But now, looking back, I could see how utterly foolish I was.

It was the third day since the envoy left. Serafina had been acting strange since morning, sneaking in naps between her duties.

I figured she must be tired, but that was odd as well—if anything, her work that day was far less taxing today than the day before. Had her fatigue finally caught up with her? Soon enough, I was relieved to learn that we had an early departure tomorrow, and she had been taking naps to ensure that she was rested.

The planned expedition was a five-day trip to the Barbizet duchy that neighbored the Royal Capital. Serafina's older sister, the first princess, had married into the Barbizet duke family.

Our visit was half-political: It allowed the nobles to witness the Great Saint's might by showcasing Serafina fighting monsters alongside knights. But the visit also allowed Serafina a much-needed rest, and it deepened her ties with the Duchess of Barbizet—or, to put it less formally, the visit gave her time to spend with her sister. The two had been close since childhood.

I was certain Serafina was looking forward to the visit, as she had set our departure for sunrise.

The next morning, she appeared in a light-blue dress. I thought the dress suited her well but was surprised to see that she chose one so unadorned. On a visit to her older sister, she usually wore an extravagant dress covered in frills and laces, something you'd expect for a princess. I felt a sense of unease, as if something was wrong...but I was no authority on women's dresses and so convinced myself this must simply be the current style that was "in these days," as they say.

Serafina and her ladies-in-waiting slowly boarded their coach, and a second wave of unease came over me. Why was she so eager to nap at every spare moment yesterday if she could simply nap in the coach? The answer came sooner than I'd expected.

We'd just left the Royal Castle and arrived at the busiest crossing when Serafina's coach came to an abrupt halt. The knights escorting her, positioned to encircle the coach, hurriedly stopped as well. I immediately dismounted my horse and opened the door of the coach to check what was wrong...and for Serafina to burst out onto the road.

She looked up at a knight in front of her and smiled. "Forgive me, but could you come down for a brief moment?"

The knight was confused, naturally, but couldn't refuse a request from a princess. No sooner had he dismounted, however, did Serafina hop onto the saddle in one swift motion, briefly revealing not the flat and narrow slippers one would expect beneath her dress, but—to my utter shock—boots fit for horseback.

Beaming, she loudly proclaimed, "The Barbizet duchy is nice and all, but I think I'll pass on it this time. I'm rather in the mood for seeing the ocean right now. There's a letter in the coach, along with a gift for my sister, so let's have about half of you knights deliver that for me. She's a pretty strong saint in her own right, so I'm sure she can do the demonstration for the nobles in my stead. As a matter of fact, it turned out better—that way, the nobles will learn of the duchess's strength. I already said as much in my letter, so make sure that gets to her, pretty please? Now, then...where should I go?" In an exaggerated manner, she put a finger to her cheek and tilted her head.

All the knights present looked at her with glassy eyes. Being Serafina's escort, they were elites, meaning they could very well predict the words about to come out of her mouth.

"Oh...I know!" She smacked her fist against her palm. "There's no place better than Sutherland if you want to see the ocean! Yes, I think I'll go to Sutherland! All right, team—split up, and my half will follow me...to Sutherland!"

Unsure what to say or do in response to her theatrics, everybody simply stared blankly at her.

Unfortunately, Serafina had made a blunder there. She wanted half of the knights to go to the duchy of Barbizet and the other half to follow her to the earldom of Sutherland, but she didn't tell them *who* should go *where*. So, instead of half-and-half, the majority of the knights followed Serafina, and only a scanty group went with the coach. I could only pray that the duchess wouldn't misunderstand and believe the Kingdom was showing her the proper respect.

One of Serafina's shortcomings was her inability to recognize her own popularity.

The journey to Sutherland was more grueling than any of the knights could've imagined when they chose to come along. For we had only five days to travel there and back again.

We used a route typically reserved for messengers, exchanging our horses with those Serafina had preemptively ordered prepared at relay stations along the way. Our numbers were far greater than the half she'd expected, but the station manager had the forethought to prepare extra horses just in case.

The more experienced riders with large frames rode in front of her. They were to serve as windbreakers to reduce the burden on her and to make sure that the path she traveled was safe.

Surprisingly, she took hardly any breaks at all. Every time we exchanged horses, she downed some water, ate something light, and then reaffixed her saddle and urged us to take off once more.

Though she was the Great Saint, her stamina couldn't be any greater than that of any other lady's—yet not once did she complain as she tightly clutched her reins.

We reached Sutherland the night of the second day, just before the break of dawn. The ones who showed symptoms of the yellow-speckle fever were quarantined at the lord's mansion, so we hurried there.

There was little space within the mansion, so many people were forced to stay in the courtyard. Some sat up with worry upon hearing the uncommon sounds of horses arriving—riders rarely arrived in the dark of night, and rarer still with good intentions. The townspeople roused one after another, watching with naked fear as we opened the mansion gates.

The few small bonfires scattered across the courtyard provided just enough light to show that we were knights, but not enough to make out the color of our uniforms. None could discern the red of the Great Saint's Royal Guard. Realizing that, I thought I would reassure everyone by revealing my identity, but Serafina slipped off her horse and approached them before I could.

She reached out to a baby that had begun to cry, startled by the sudden commotion. The baby's mother looked up at Serafina, amazed. At the sight of Serafina's gentle smile, she handed the baby to her.

Serafina held the baby tenderly and, in a soft, almost sing-song voice, said, "My, you've hung in there so well for such a little thing. What a strong baby you are."

Tears began to fall from the mother's eyes. "Ah, th-thank you. A-all the other mainlanders won't even approach us out of fear of the disease."

Just then, a number of people approached with torches, illuminating Serafina's hair.

"Th-the Great Saint?!"

"I-It couldn't be..."

Serafina certainly wasn't the only woman in this world with red hair, but the people knew of their chief's request. Who else, they thought, would arrive like this in the dead of night?

Murmurs of surprise and wonder began to break out. By this point, none were asleep—everyone was on their feet, or at least sitting up as best they could, staring at Serafina with eyes full of expectation.

She took in all their gazes and smiled. "Yes, it is I, Serafina Náv the Great Saint." She kissed the cheek of the baby in her arms. The spot she kissed began to shine radiantly, and the pattern of yellow speckles faded from the baby's body.

"What? My baby's healed?" muttered the mother as she received her baby.

Everyone stared in speechless astonishment. Serafina then lifted an arm toward the sky and augustly said, "Oh, ye bountiful and rich earth of Sutherland, grant your blessing to the loyal, meek peoples of your land. As the fire purifies, as the wind buffets, as the water washes away, let to your earth smother this contaminant within—*Cleanse Sickness.*"

A brilliant light began to gleam from her extended fingers. It overwhelmed the light of the bonfires, the torches, the stars—all that had lit up the night—and shone with a reddish tinge. Abruptly, the light leapt upward and split above the heads of the townspeople.

"Huh? Wh-what is this?"

The townspeople stared at the night sky, surprise plain on their faces. They watched in awe as grains of light drifted down, as if the stars themselves had inexplicably fallen from the sky. As those grains of light touched the townspeople, they began to exclaim in wonder.

"I-It's so warm."

The grains of light disappeared on contact as though melting, spreading a sudden warmth through the air. Soon the townspeople cupped their hands as they stared at the sky, as if to catch a pool of falling water, and tried to capture the falling light.

The townspeople were convinced that the light was the warm, pure love of the Great Saint, and they wished with all their hearts to receive it. The shining grains filled them with a sense of comfort and safety on touch, so they focused on nothing but catching the lights. Only once the last grain of light was gone and the courtyard had returned to darkness did the townspeople return to their senses and realize the change that had overtaken their bodies.

"I...I can't believe it. Th-they're gone."

"Th-the yellow speckles are gone. My fever's gone too."

"It can't be... Did she heal us all, and so quickly?"

The townspeople all checked themselves over before looking back at Serafina, speechless. They couldn't believe someone could heal their incurable disease, with such speed.

Serafina merely smiled, unaffected by their stares, before suddenly buckling over slightly. I rushed over and saw the sweat clinging to the back of her dress. She hadn't relied on the spirits to cast her spell just now—to perform this feat, she'd drained herself completely of magic.

Worried, the townspeople approached with torches, illuminating Serafina. Now that I could see her, I knew that she was not in good shape by any standards. The hem of her dress was covered in kicked-up mud, and her garments were wrinkled all over from two days of wear. If Serafina's sister, the first princess—or any noblewoman, for that matter—were to be in such a state, they'd promptly insist that they were unpresentable and rush away to change.

The dawn began to break over the crowd. The dark sky brightened as the sun rose—one single beam of light fell upon them, followed by another, painting the sky a deep red. The light shone on Serafina from behind, a scarlet halo. The light of dawn mingled with the red of her hair, one indistinguishable from the other.

"The Great Saint of Dawn..." a townsperson murmured with a trembling voice.

"She's the light itself...the beautiful red light that casts away the darkness..." murmured another townsperson, overcome with emotion.

Indeed, Serafina looked divine as she stood in the darkness with a spotlight on her. The crowd seemed to shiver as one, their throat gone dry and goosebumps on their skin. It was as though a line from a myth had been recreated before their very eyes. One by one, they all took a knee.

Yes...she is beautiful. Beautiful, benevolent, and a savior to all.

Everyone understood the fate that had awaited the former islanders. Our people had been on track to die from the disease, wiped out completely. But the Great Saint herself had turned that fate away, saving everyone—young and old.

That salvation was only made possible by Serafina's kind heart. The journey to Sutherland was ten days by coach. Even though she opted to use a horse, she'd still covered the distance in two days... It was hard to fathom. Not once did she complain as she rode, fighting sleepiness and fatigue all the way. She didn't give a single thought to the dangers of falling off her horse, instead devoting herself wholly to reaching my people. Her body must have ached with unbearable pain, and yet she used all of her magic for the people.

Out of both magic and stamina, she should've hardly had it in her to stand. Her mind must've been hazy. Even so, she smiled from the bottom of her heart. She was overjoyed to save these people, overjoyed that they could live and smile again. This was the true identity of the Great Saint everyone worshipped.

By the time I realized it, the thousands of townspeople were on their knees. As though worshipping something divine, they lowered their heads. They wept and prayed. But not a one could utter a word—the gratitude was too great for mere words.

Today it begins, I thought. No matter how many years passed— it could be a century or a millennium—my people would worship Serafina as their savior for as long as they lived.

Oh, Great Saint, the most beautiful and benevolent of them all... You are on your way to becoming a legend.

Afterward, after asking the still-excited townspeople for permission, I showed the tired Serafina to the parlor room.

I still had an important task to finish: taking the blame for her change in schedule. Serafina tried to assume all responsibility with her dramatic speech a couple days ago, but the responsibility still fell to me. I was her personal knight, after all.

When she announced her intent to go to Sutherland, I was surprised...but I was also overjoyed and grateful. The people of Sutherland were my people; I wanted them saved if at all possible. I believed there was nothing I could do to save them myself, so when Serafina acted, I was delighted and made no effort to stop her.

I helped Serafina sit down in a chair and performed the knight salute before her. "Your Highness, I accept all blame for failing to stop you from visiting Sutherland. I knew the journey would be dangerous, but I foolishly refrained from admonishing you out of concern for the lives of my people. Please, forgive this foolish knight of yours."

She looked up at me and tilted her head. "Huh? Didn't I say I wanted to come see the ocean? I'm the only one at fault here."

"Your Highness, please! Not a single person was deceived by your poor acting!"

"Whaaaat? That hurts. But I'll just insist I *wasn't* acting. I just wanted to see the ocean!"

"I tell you, nobody is going to believe that! Your Highness, how many times must I repeat myself before you learn?!"

She looked up at me again with a phony, meek expression. "Forgive me for failing to learn, Canopus. I must cause you so much grief."

"Your Highness! Please...spare me the act! Jeez...how can the peerless Great Saint be such a headache?!" Frustrated with her insistence on taking responsibility, I accidentally voiced my true thoughts.

I was hesitating over whether to even continue this discussion when she smiled. "I'm sorry for being such a handful, but I simply had to see your territory as soon as possible. That's why I was in a bit of a rush."

"A bit? A bit?!" I couldn't help but break into a peal of laughter. "You call riding full tilt for two days without rest, changing horses as you go...that's 'a bit'?! In what world?!"

I intended to keep the conversation focused on who would bear responsibility for the visit, but I couldn't refrain from challenging her words. Over the course of the journey, she'd had a number of close calls that almost gave me heart attacks—branches had nearly smacked her right in the face, her horse had been stuck in mud...all kinds of trouble.

"I'm sorry," she said.

I thought she would reprimand me, as my tone was harsher than I intended, but to my surprise, she seemed despondent. I sighed, cursing my immaturity, and knelt before her. "Your Highness, there is no one who I value more highly in this world. I beg you, before you do anything rash again, think about my own purpose. I am your personal knight. I exist to serve and protect you."

"I know. From the bottom of my heart, Canopus...I apologize for being so impulsive."

I sighed. I knew she felt bad for her actions, but I also knew she'd do it again in a heartbeat, if presented with the same opportunity. And she wouldn't tell me beforehand, either—she knew I'd try to stop her. But her safety was more important to me than anything. She knew this too, of course, and so she acted rashly, all while trying to prevent any responsibility from falling upon me.

I sighed again, much more deeply this time, and looked Serafina squarely in the eyes. I figured I'd leave things at that for today. Our discussion wasn't getting anywhere, and she was quite tired. It was time to wrap up the conversation.

"As long as you understand," I said. I bowed deeply enough for my head to touch the ground. "I am deeply humbled to have Her Holiness Great Saint, the Second Princess Serafina Náv, pay a visit to my territory. I, and all of my people, welcome you with open arms."

Of course, my words didn't even begin to express the gratitude my people felt for her.

I then addressed the smiling townspeople who were peering through the door—I'd left it open a crack out of politeness. "Prepare a welcome party at once. We must show our gratitude to Her Holiness." They scattered quickly; no doubt overjoyed at the prospect of holding a celebration for the Great Saint.

I extended a hand to Serafina in order to help her up, and I guided her back to the courtyard. "If it's all right, would you be willing to appear before everyone again?" I asked her. "I'm sure everyone would like a chance to see you one more time."

"Yes, gladly! I'd like to meet them as well."

She was no doubt exhausted, but—with the townspeople's excitement nearly palpable—there was no way she would rest even if I begged. The best I could do was make her sit down and eat while she enjoyed herself. Before long, she would surely run out of energy and fall asleep on her own.

The moment we entered the courtyard, the townspeople began to crowd around Serafina.

"Your Holiness, thank you for saving us!"

"Thank you for saving my little brother, Your Holiness!"

"Your Holiness, I heard you were extremely busy, but thank you for visiting despite your disheveled appearance!"

"W-wait, what was that last one?!" Serafina exclaimed. "Do I look all right?! O-oh, no, how unbecoming of me!" She frantically tried to brush her hair, bringing a smile to peoples' faces.

The crowd fawned over her. "Your appearance is proof of the lengths you went for us! Surely no other royalty is as beautiful, noble, and full of love as you!"

"Even if we die out one day, our people will remember our loyalty to you until the last person!"

Serafina made an uncomfortable smile. "Uhh, I only just did what I could. A chef cooks, right? Well, I'm a saint, so I heal. That's all there is to it."

Not a single person agreed with her.

Perhaps she wasn't *wrong*, exactly. Any saint would heal another if they could...but no other saint that I knew of would risk their life riding on horseback for two days straight just to heal someone.

To cure the mutated yellow-speckle fever variant, one had to understand the workings of the disease and create a spell that could work against it. And I found myself certain that only Serafina was capable of such a thing.

Lady Serafina, just how much dedication and practice did you go through in order to reach such incredible heights?

Although the townspeople did not know how much work Serafina put into her duties, they understood that no one achieved greatness by doing nothing. Her talents were the fruits of her own effort, proof that she worked harder than anyone else in the land.

A crowd of children ran up and surrounded her. "Your Holiness! We heard you're busy and have to leave soon. Please come visit again!"

"Yeah! Sutherland's ocean is really nice! Please come swim in it next time."

"Mmh! The sun makes the white walls of our town all shiny! Come see it soon!"

The children continued to beg her to visit again. At that, Serafina tilted her head slightly and laughed. She scanned her eyes across the courtyard, then walked to a tree planted by the side and broke off a young branch.

"Is it all right if I plant this cutting to commemorate my visit?" she asked.

The children quickly replied, eyes glittering with joy. "Plant it right in the middle of the courtyard!"

"Yeah! Right in the center where no one can miss it!"

Serafina didn't seem sure. "Oh...but won't it get in the way?"

I broke in. "Lady Serafina, by all means, please plant it in the center. If anything, take it as a request from me, the owner of this estate."

"My, Canopus!" she teased. "And here I thought it was your job to warn me when I crossed the line like this."

I grinned. "What would be the point? You never heed my warnings in the first place. Regardless, I'd like you to plant it in the center so people can gather around it for ages to come."

She succumbed to both the pleading of the kids and my insistence. Together with the children, we planted the branch in the middle of the courtyard. The children then happily patted the dirt around the branch and watered the earth.

Serafina, satisfied, faced the children. "This small branch comes from an adela tree. Do you children know what an adela tree is?"

"I know! It's a tree with super pretty red flowers!"

"Yeah, and now's the season they bloom. Look! You can see the flowers right now!"

Serafina turned around and looked at the tree she took the branch from, joy bright in her eyes. "Yes, they are in bloom. It's warm in Sutherland, so the trees bloom earlier than in the Royal Capital. Heh heh, I guess I came at just the right time."

As she continued to admire the adela flowers, the children began to list off everything they knew about them.

"The red flowers smell nice!"

"They're such a pretty kinda red, Your Holiness! Like your hair!"

Serafina nodded with admiration and gently patted the children's heads. "My, you all know so much. How about this? Around the time this tree grows big and blooms pretty red flowers that remind everyone of me, then I'll come and visit Sutherland again."

The children, as well as the adults listening in behind them, cried out with glee as one. "Your Holiness!"

She smiled, held her hand to the side of her head, and impishly extended a pinky. "It's my promise to everyone."

She made a promise to revisit Sutherland, fully intent on fulfilling it. But in the end, her promise went unfulfilled...

The preparations for the celebration went quickly. The towns-people hurried, knowing that Serafina couldn't stay long and that this celebration would be their only chance to show her a warm welcome.

In a corner of the courtyard, a colorful cloth was laid out with a number of fine embroidered cushions stacked atop.

Serafina's eyes sparkled at the sight of the cushions. "Ooh, these are the traditional crafts of the former islanders, right? They're beautiful!" The people were happy to hear it—who doesn't like hearing praise for one's culture?

Smiling, the townspeople led her to take a seat. The moment she sat down, they began carrying food out, starting with what could be easily prepared. The foods included bread baked last night that had been meant for breakfast, a salad made from vegetables picked just this morning, and a soup left simmering overnight with freshly roasted meat. There was even a fish that was typically cooked through a long simmer until it was nice and soft, but here it's served after a light grill instead.

"My, everything looks so delicious!" said Serafina enthusiastically. "I haven't properly eaten these last two days, so I think I'll be able to eat quite a lot today! Thank you, everyone."

"There's no greater honor than for Her Holiness to eat our food! The chefs are cooking away in the kitchen as we speak, so there's still much more food to come."

"Wonderful!" said Serafina and right away began digging

into an egg dish. I gasped at that and prepared to rush at her, but she shot me a look and whispered to me "Don't worry, I drank a magic restoration potion."

You see, members of the royal family were always at risk of being poisoned. Serafina, as the second princess, was no exception. But as a powerful saint, she was effectively immune to it. The moment she took them in, her saint powers activated and cleansed the poison—whether or not she was even aware of it. However, this power couldn't activate when she was out of magic. Although she'd just had a magic restoration potion, it was the sort that promised a slow, gradual recovery. What if she didn't have enough magic to neutralize a poison?

Ignoring my worries, Serafina hungrily ate away at the food, trying a bit of every dish.

To me, it was oh-so-clear what she was doing. For this many dishes to be prepared in such a short time meant there had to be many chefs at work, and an even greater number of people who had provided the ingredients. Out of consideration for each and every one of those people, she was trying as much as she could...which also meant that the risk of being poisoned was much higher.

I watched warily as she devoured the food. I made sure not to even blink.

"What's with the frown, Canopus?" she asked suddenly. "Come, sit with me."

I'd typically refuse such a request, but this time I accepted and sat diagonally behind her—this was a good opportunity to protect her from up close. As the lord of Sutherland, it wouldn't be taken as an act of disrespect to be so close to my charge as I served her.

No sooner had I sat down did I spot the chief of the townspeople running over. The chief didn't stay at the mansion, as he wasn't infected with the yellow-speckle fever. He'd probably run straight here, all the way from home.

He stopped before Serafina and prostrated himself, his head grazing the ground. "Your Holiness, thank you for saving our people. I swear we will remember your benevolence with gratitude for all eternity."

"You're the chief, aren't you?" she asked. "Please, raise your head. I'm the one who should be thankful. Thank you for leading your people as one of the pillars of our country. It's only natural that I save my own citizens, but that wouldn't be possible without people like you. We can only do what must be done because we support one another."

In contrast to Serafina's easy smile, the chief was rendered momentarily speechless, as if overcome with emotion. "S-s-such kind words..." he at last managed to say. "T-to think you would call us citizens of your own. Support one another...y-yes! Yes, I swear that our people shall never fight with anyone from the mainland from this day on. We'll live in harmony with all, relying on one another as one!"

Serafina blinked. "Okay, although I think it'd be all right to quarrel if something *really* bothers you, you know? Even I can't help but argue with Canopus here from time to time."

Wait, why would Serafina say something like *that* out of the blue? Totally uncalled for. Perhaps the chief's zeal overtook her, and she let it slip, but...well, no reason to ruin the heaps of praise she was receiving by saying anything about it.

I did frown, though. Heavily.

She just giggled. Happily.

"Hey, chief, did you know Canopus is really kind? After we argue, he always makes sure to reflect on what he said and apologize. Sometimes I wonder why we argue, but in the end, I always realize he's doing it for my sake. This peaceful, plentiful land raised such a kindhearted man. Thank you, chief, for sending my wonderful knight to me."

The chief and I were speechless. Serafina was positively unfair! Just what was I supposed to say after being praised so grandly? The chief looked at me with deep envy in his eyes.

"L-Lady Serafina..." I began, lost for words but unable to bear the silence any longer.

"Oh!" Without hesitation, she moved on. "That's right, chief. Since I healed the yellow-speckle fever from everyone earlier, I ran my healing magic through them. Now I completely understand the disease. I can make special healing potions for it, so I'll do just that and send them here to you once I return to the Royal Castle. It should be enough to heal people if the disease ever pops up again, as long as the symptoms haven't advanced too far."

"Th-thank you so very much!" the chief stammered. "I-I can't begin to thank you enough for all that you've done for us!" Once again, the chief's head met the ground.

I really don't think he needed to prostrate himself *that* much, although I understood how he felt. The Great Saint, said to be the Kingdom's greatest treasure, had done so much for Sutherland. She'd pushed herself to ride to Sutherland until she could hardly stand, cured an incurable disease that would've annihilated our people, passionately defended our value as citizens of the Kingdom from the never-ending onslaught of discrimination, and even shown consideration for our future by promising to send medicine for those who might be afflicted by the disease in the future.

Yes...I could see it, then. Just like all the others she has healed so far, the chief and all my people would undoubtedly worship the noble, benevolent Great Saint with all of their hearts.

Just as I let out a heavy, emotional sigh, the first notes of a song rang out. A dance demonstration for Serafina had begun. For the opening performance, children lined up and danced wearing the colorful folk clothing of the former islanders.

Serafina watched the children with sparkling eyes. "Aw, they're so cute! Hmm...ah, yes! This has gotta be a jellyfish dance," she said confidently.

"I'm impressed you were able to guess they were mimicking an aquatic animal," I said evenly. "Unfortunately, they are mimicking dolphins, not jellyfish."

"O-oh! Well, uh...I'm not *wrong*, though, if you think about it. Same thing, basically. Falls under the umbrella. "

"Hmm...forgive me, but the umbrella you speak of sounds impossibly large."

The townspeople interrupted before Serafina could defend her position on marine life. "Your Holiness, we have more food for you! This is one of our traditional foods, a deep-sea shellfish baked with flour!"

"My, this is my first time seeing such a dish," said Serafina. "How deep do you have to go to find this shellfish?"

"Only our most experienced adult divers can reach them. With our webbed fingers, our people have exclusive access to deep-sea shellfish that no one else can reach."

"My, my! These shellfish must be incredibly rare then. Let me try one...*nom!* Oh, it's delicious! It's got a peculiar chewiness, some bitterness too, but it comes together so beautifully! Oh, I could eat this dish every day. What do you call it?" she asked, eyes sparkling.

The townsperson smiled proudly. *"Oatsun!"*

"Oachun. Got it."

"Ha! Not quite, Your Holiness."

As everyone laughed together, a few small children approached. "Your Holiness, this flower's for you!"

"Your Holiness, I made you a garland. It's yellow, so I think it'll look good on your red hair."

The children had clearly taken bunches of flowers from the estate's flowerbed.

I'll...just pretend I didn't see anything. I could imagine the veins bulging in the gardener's face already, but I quickly shook the thought away. Serafina was having fun, and the townspeople looked happy. I could overlook something like this.

Just as the children's dance came to an end and the next dancers began to take the stage, everyone noticed Serafina was lying down on her cushion. In her hands and on her head were the flowers and garland the children brought her. All at once, she had fallen asleep.

"She lasted longer than I expected," I mused. "She's ridden on horseback for two straight days and pushed herself with magic till it was gone. She's hit her limit, so please allow her to rest."

Nobody objected. Afterward, I thoroughly enjoyed the dances they offered her in her stead.

But soon enough, it was time. I lifted Serafina up, and the townspeople ran toward us with a start. "As sad as I am to say it, it is time for Her Holiness to be on her way. We only have two and a half days to return. Lady Serafina expressed that she wished she could stay half a day longer, but I cannot allow such a thing—it would mean putting her in harm's way with another exhausting two-day ride."

After explaining, I put a foot in the stirrup of the horse I had prepared and climbed on, still holding Serafina in my arms. "While I'm a little reluctant to ride two people on one horse, even with the extra time afforded, Her Holiness is too exhausted as it is. She'll likely be out for a full day, so I'll hold on to her for the duration."

"Ohhh! Lord Canopus will hold Her Holiness for the two and a half days it takes to reach the castle, then? I see. Please take extra care not to drop Her Holiness, Lord Canopus!"

I couldn't help but frown at the townsperson's words. *Ah, so it's already begun.*

I stiffened my expression. "Did you listen properly to what I said? I'll be riding while holding onto Her Holiness for *one* whole day, not two and a half. Perhaps you all haven't realized, but I also haven't slept once in these past two and a half days. Don't you think you're expecting a little much from me?"

"But Lord Canopus, you're a knight, and a knight must protect their princess! You said it yourself: Her Holiness is exhausted! Let her rest! I'm sure you can handle two more days without sleeping!"

Ah, there it is, there it is. Faced with the sudden change in behavior of the townspeople, I frowned. The adoration and respect they'd treated me with on my last visit had vanished in an instant. They showed no hesitation now in encouraging me to run myself ragged for Serafina's sake. I'd seen similar instances many times before, but I never expected it from my own brethren and subjects...

I shook my head, appalled, and tried one last ditch effort to improve my situation. "Oh, I don't know. I don't think I can hold on to Her Holiness for two and a half days for a total of five days straight without sleep—"

Despite being the lord, I was immediately interrupted. "Don't be a coward! Just look how small Her Holiness is! She managed to push herself to ride two full days without sleep or rest! You're many times her weight, so can't you go many times as long?!"

"Many times as...?! Listen, I don't know where you got the idea from, but there's no correlation whatsoever between body weight and stamina," I said, appalled that I even had to explain such a thing. Sadly, nobody was on my side.

"I'm disappointed in you, Lord Canopus! I didn't think you were the kind of man to complain about missing a little sleep!"

"A *little* sleep? Two days! I rode here on horseback for two full days, and you're telling me to do it again without any rest! Do you hear yourselves?!" But nobody heard a word. It was on to the next subject: my next visit.

"Lord Canopus, you absolutely must bring Her Holiness with you when you next visit!"

"Yes, you must!"

"Wh-what?! No, I can't! Her Holiness is always very busy. Besides, that tree's flowers won't bloom for quite some time." I began getting defensive, overwhelmed by the fervor of the townspeople.

"Then you must stay by Her Holiness's side and protect her always!"

"Yes, you mustn't let anything happen to her! Stay close to her always and protect her in our stead!"

These people, I swear. "*Gaah!* I can't believe my own subjects are insisting I don't return to my own territory without bringing Her Holiness along!" I'd meant my words as a joke, but my subjects nodded back approvingly.

"I'd expect no less from you, Lord Canopus! You understand us so well!"

"We look forward to your return with Her Holiness!"

"..."

And so, it was decided: I could not return to *my own* territory unless I had Serafina with me.

With a belabored sigh, I said farewell to everyone and began to ride away. As I left, and even after they faded from view, everyone continued to thank Serafina—and didn't offer a word of thanks to me.

I looked down at her in my arms and saw her snoring quietly. Dark rings had formed under her eyes, and her hand was rough from holding her reins. I sighed again, exhausted.

Always so reckless, always pushing herself so hard. Where would she be without me to protect her?

I looked up at the cloudless sky and thought back to the events of the past few hours. I thought back to her divine figure under the light of dawn after she saved all the townspeople and remembered the sweet smile on her face as she praised me. From the bottom of my heart, I believed I served a wonderful Lady. Merely being by her side was a true blessing.

Memories from the day I became Serafina's personal knight came to mind. On that day, the vice commander gave me a few words to steel my heart as he handed me an excellent sword.

"To guard the royal family, you must be willing to give up your life at any moment. I hope you won't place your life before that of Her Highness."

I remember what I thought then, that such devotion goes without saying. *I am prepared to offer up my life for Serafina. My life is nothing next to hers.*

But even in my darkest nightmares, I never could have imagined that I would fail in that vow...and leave Serafina to die alone...

Reality is always crueler than we expect, is it not? In the long, empty days of my life, I continued to make the same hopeless vow again and again.

"If I could be reborn and serve you once again, I would get it right. I would protect you from everything and everyone in this cruel world."

That vow became my prayer, a wish for my own salvation. Every day, I repeated this vow, until the release of death came for me...or so I had believed.

Perhaps all my life until then had only been a dream.

Perhaps my life *now* is the dream.

Within this dream where I now live, I worked together with a red-haired, golden-eyed female knight. For some reason or another, the townspeople of this time had come to think of this red-haired knight as *her* reincarnation. Even I began to think that yes, the color of her hair and the brightness of her eyes were correct, that yes, her personality was similar, when suddenly, I could not find her anywhere. Apprehensive, I searched for her until I found her surrounded by people in an alleyway. I stepped forward, thinking she was about to be abducted, but the abductors' own clumsiness got the better of them. Just as I felt relieved, the red-haired knight nonchalantly began to follow her would-be abductors. I thought she was insane. I carefully tailed them, reminding myself to warn her sternly later, and we all ended up in a cave.

Something snapped in me, then. Watching them lead the red-haired knight into this dim cave brought me back to that long eternity, those ages of wondering what horrors *she* might've suffered. My mind seemed to awaken from its slumber, my thoughts vivid and bright, as the world I had felt I was only watching from a distance, as if peering in through a window, began to become sharper and become clear before my eyes. Something within my chest stirred, and my emotions became my own once more.

"I... Who am I? What...is my purpose?" I asked myself this over and over in my mind, but before an answer could come, a stronger thought rose above the confusion. *"I have to save her! I must protect her from everything and everyone in this cruel world!"*

I will not lose her again!

A memory rose in my mind of long days spent in emptiness and despair. A bone-chilling cold assailed me. The memories... were they mine? Or did they belong to someone else? A fierce headache came on, and a wave of nausea...

Calm down, Kurtis. These memories, all these days full of despair...they aren't mine. They can't be. But...who?! That calm, rational part of my mind was rapidly being overwhelmed by the memories.

My body moved on its own, hurriedly drawing its sword and attacking the townspeople, and I imagined that this was a dream. It had to be a dream.

In no time at all, I was cut down.

"Ah...once again, I couldn't protect you."

Moments before I lost consciousness, I saw the female knight looking at me worriedly. That dawn-like hair and golden eyes...

This must be a dream. A dream where I lose her again. When next I open my eyes, I'll return to those endless days... I'll awake to the cold regret and the guilt that ruled my life.

"Get...back...Lady...se...fi...a..." My head throbbed and my words, barely muttered with the last of my failing strength, faded away into the wind.

A Tale of the
Secret
Saint

28

The Visit to Sutherland Part 3

"**C**APTAIN KURTIS!" I screamed.

He lay motionless on the ground, eyes closed and pale from blood loss. He would surely die without aid. I knelt and touched his body, discreetly healing him while leaving the surface of his wounds open. Maybe I could've woken him, but...no, it'd probably be better to wait for him to awaken naturally.

Still touching Kurtis's body, I turned to face Ariel and glared. "He may have drawn his sword first, but you went too far! Even if you were trying to protect the sick!"

Ariel looked bewildered. "N-no, Your Holiness, we were trying to protect you! That knight drew his blade and made a beeline for you, looking all menacing! We did what we had to!"

"Huh?! Her Holiness? Me?! U-um, I'm not the Great—" Oh, wait, right. This time I was *supposed* to be me. "I mean, um, I might be the Great Saint? But what makes you think I am, anyway?"

Ariel and the others hadn't shown any sign they thought I was the Great Saint until now, so I'd assumed they hadn't heard all the rumors going around.

"Well, you have dawn-like red hair, and the expression on your face when you saw those people…it was like you knew they were sick at a glance. The moment I—no, we saw that face, we were sure you were the Great Saint who promised to one day return."

Ariel and all the other guards prostrated themselves, touching their heads to the ground in apology. "We're sorry for not realizing you were the Great Saint earlier! We should have known from your brilliant hair alone! Forgive us!"

"Like hell!" a voice roared.

I spun around to see Kurtis, who definitely should have been out cold, propping himself up and glaring at Ariel. Blood oozed from his wounds, and his face was deathly pale, but his eyes held a new and fierce will.

"You bastards committed an unforgivable act of violence against Her Holiness!" he growled. "Remember all she has done for the people of Sutherland! Once you've done that, then pray for forgiveness! I promise only to make your deaths swift and painless!" With that, Kurtis grabbed his sword and got into position, ready to protect me.

Something seemed…*off* about Kurtis.

Uhh, who are you? He looked like himself, and yet something was palpably different. Up until he'd reawakened, he was far and away the weakest of the captains, but now he seemed to have a strength I just couldn't gauge. It was like staring into the un-fathomable depths of still, clear waters. Or perhaps it would be better to describe his strength as an endless abyss of unknowable vastness. Either way, I'd met people like that in my past life. There were those whose strength I couldn't read at first glance, and all of them had proved frighteningly powerful...

I stared at Kurtis, making doubly sure that my eyes weren't fooling me, when I realized he was exuding killing intent. I quickly stood up to grab his arm. "C-calm down, Captain Kurtis! I know you want to get back at them for what they did to you, but please refrain! C'mon, behave yourself and I'm sure your wounds will heal up nice and quick!"

He looked back at me, flummoxed. "Where do I even begin..."

"S-sorry?" I said, confused.

"I intend to do away with those men not as revenge but as punishment for their actions toward you. Whatever they do to me is secondary... Even if they were to kill me, I'd feel no resent-ment whatsoever."

"Huh?"

"Furthermore, my current wounds haven't healed because I've *behaved myself.* You healed them."

"Wha-huh?" I stared into his eyes, shocked...and he blinked. Twice.

I froze. A calm voice inside my head fought against my racing heart. *That can't be. It's impossible. Calm down.* But no matter how I tried, I couldn't get that familiar habit of his out of my mind. That double blink belonged to a man from my past life. A man who'd always blinked twice when meeting my eyes, as though he were looking at something dazzling. But...no, it couldn't be...

My thoughts in chaos, I stared at him hard. His expression immediately became troubled. That was the same too... Those quickly downcast eyes from three hundred years ago were exactly the same.

It's him. It's him. It's him. Even the calm voice inside my head betrayed itself now.

Because I stared at him so dumbfounded, he made an uncomfortable face and sheathed his sword. The way he moved...

It's him. It's him. It's him... It has to be him. Even without any logic or proof, my mind was full of conviction. Unable to resist any longer, I spoke in a trembling voice. "I...thought I'd be able to visit your grave in Sutherland. I can't... I couldn't find it. I tried, but I couldn't."

Kurtis smiled sadly. "I believe a grave is where the heart returns to rest, so I asked that mine be placed next to the demon lord's castle. You see, it was a tomb...the tomb of the only liege I've had the honor to serve."

Tears began to stream from my eyes. Flustered, he quickly knelt before me and extended his hands, but hesitated, uncertain whether or not to wipe my face. But not even his awkward efforts could do anything to stop my tears.

"It's you..." I whispered. And I addressed him by name for the first time in three hundred years. "Canopus."

"Yes, my lady."

The moment I heard his response, fresh tears came streaming down.

"Canopus…Canopus…Canopus…"

"Yes…yes…yes, I'm here."

I took a deep breath and yelled, "Canopus!" I fell to the ground then and buried my face in my hands, weeping.

Canopus became flustered and hesitated again—to wipe my tears or not? As single-mindedly loyal as he was, he never touched me unless I ordered it.

"Pfft, ha ha, Canopus…" I couldn't help but laugh through the tears. So exceedingly earnest, even three hundred years later…

Reluctantly, he offered me a handkerchief. "This handkerchief is far too plain for someone of your status," he mumbled, "but feel free to make use of it if you so please."

Still crying, I grabbed his extended hand with my own. "Thank you, Canopus. For returning to me."

"Of course, my lady," he answered, looking far too serious.

He always did, though. And only then, seeing his stern face, was I completely certain, from the bottom of my heart. *It really is you.* To think I would one day be reunited with my exceedingly earnest and loyal-to-a-fault personal knight…

Canopus was still flustered and hovered around me uncertainly, but eventually, my tears came to an end.

Oh, dear Canopus. I wonder if you even realize the precious sight of you is the reason I'm crying!

After–action Report for the Sojourn to Sutherland

(THREE HUNDRED YEARS AGO)

"**O**H? I BELIEVE I CALLED for my little sister, and yet what do I see before me but a dirty maidservant?" My older brother, Vega, the first prince, gave me a look of mocking surprise. I sighed quietly. Behind me, I could hear my personal knight, Canopus, grind his teeth.

The first thing I did after returning from Sutherland to the Royal Castle was head to my brother Vega's office. I bore responsibility for my decision to go to Sutherland. Being the Great Saint, one of the Kingdom's most precious treasures, my schedule was determined by the Kingdom's Supreme Council—composed of the princes, chancellor, and ministers. By going to the Sutherland earldom instead of the Barbizet duchy, I'd essentially abandoned their plan without warning. For that reason, I was going straight to Vega, the Council's representative, to apologize...and yet the first thing out of his mouth were those condescending words.

Give me a break, Brother... And get that grin off your face while you're at it! You know very well I'm your sister and not some maid-servant. Why do you always have to waste time like this? Doesn't the first prince have better things to do?

Unfortunately, my internal grumblings failed to reach my brother. "Gracious me, what an unbecoming appearance. I thought commoners these days knew how to take better care of themselves, but it seems I was wrong." He looked me up and down rudely, put on a frown, then laid his arms on his desk and rested his chin in his hands.

"Now, where oh where might my sister be?" He stretched and dramatized each word like an amateur actor. "My benevo-lent, pure as a newborn, *idiotic* sister who so selfishly neglected the schedule that our Kingdom's busiest leaders slaved away to establish?"

Was he done? He was done. Finally. "Standing before you, my brother. While my hair may be dirtied beyond recognition, I assure you that I am—without a doubt—your sister Serafina."

I stood a step below the raised floor my brother's desk was on, back straight and undaunted by his attitude. My dress and hair were in a state of disarray from my rigorous five-day journey, but my mannerisms were exemplary, befitting a princess of the Kingdom. They needed to be, because I wasn't interested in suf-fering the mockeries of my brother any further.

My brother opened his eyes wide, feigning surprise. "Oh, I see! Yes, yes, that voice is unmistakably that of my idiotic sister! Did you have fun slacking off for five days, Serafina? Or did you spend your time as a beggar? You certainly look the part, ha ha ha!"

The servants behind Vega made no effort to hide their grins.

He went on. "Did you give any thought at all about those of us stuck dealing with your mess while you were goofing off? You took nearly all the knights on your little trip and sent only *four* knights to the Barbizet duchy! *Four*, Serafina! A duchy might not mean much to the oh-so-grand and noble Great Saint, but I'd say it warrants a bit more than dispatching *four damn knights* to the aristocrats!" His voice rose, dripping with still more bile. "Perhaps you don't think that the schedule the chancellor and us princes painstakingly prepared is of any importance, but I'll have you know that the Council is the highest decision-making authority there is in this Kingdom, composed of its very leaders!"

He paused for gravity. "So!" He barked. "Just where and what was *sooo* important that it made you abandon the schedule we commanded you to keep?"

I couldn't stand my brother, nor his sarcasm. Sure, I was at fault here. I'd admit that. But he didn't have to be so roundabout. I would prefer it if he just scolded me and got this all over with. He knew *exactly* where I went and what I did, but he just *had* to be a jerk about it.

I was irritated out of my mind by him, but I wouldn't shirk responsibility for my decisions. So, I looked my brother straight in the eyes and answered him. "I went to Sutherland, located at the southern tip of the Kingdom, to see the ocean. Indeed, it was a rash and imprudent decision. Forgive me." I bowed deeply in apology.

My brother was right. The visit to the Barbizet duchy was important, and I blew it off without any prior warning. The people of the Barbizet duchy were probably crestfallen to hear that I'd failed to arrive. It was precisely because he was in the right that my brother made such a condescending smirk.

"Is that right? You skipped an important national duty to see the ocean? Ha ha, ha, what can I even say? Oh, Great Saint! You have such a *unique* view of the world."

The servants behind him chuckled like hyenas.

My brother continued, glowing with self-satisfaction. "While everyone worked day and night to make up for your absence in the Barbizet duchy, you were off having a swim with your favorite knights? Wow. It must be nice, having it so easy." He grinned arrogantly, irritating me to the core.

Annoyed as I was, I had no problem with letting his sarcastic comments slide. They were nothing new, after all. Canopus behind me, on the other hand, was positively fuming. "Excuse me, but—"

Before Canopus could get another word in, my brother roared at him. "Silence, halfwit! You have no right to interrupt a conversation between royalty! Or do you long for the executioner's axe?!"

"Canopus," I said warningly. "That's enough." This whole meeting was such a hassle...

Canopus certainly knew that Vega was well aware of where I'd been and why, and that all this questioning was unnecessary. My brother just wanted to mess with me for his own amusement. But if I were to fess up and say I went to Sutherland to heal people, then the ones who'd requested my help—namely the chief, the envoy, and Canopus himself—would be punished. For that reason, I had to insist I only went for pleasure and allow my brother to have his fun, by making a fool of me.

Still, I wanted to deny him as much of that amusement as I could, so Canopus and I had to remain as calm and dignified as possible. That was hard for Canopus. He didn't like to see me mocked so viciously—his heart was too loyal. What was more, he felt a lot of responsibility for the whole matter and was more than happy to throw himself into the fire for me.

I thought back to the apology he gave me numerous times on our return from Sutherland.

"Forgive me. I've created a weakness for the princes to take advantage of."

Every time, I just smiled. *"Nonsense. Something like that is nothing compared to the lives of thousands."* Still, the look of worry never left his face.

Canopus was too earnest. I understood how he felt and why he wanted to cover for me, but the best course of action was to stay quiet and let this whole thing blow over.

Just then, I heard the door fly open behind me. I knew only one person rude enough to enter the first prince's office without so much as a knock.

"Serafina! Didn't I tell you to come straight to my place once you've returned?!"

It took all I had to refrain from praising the one who had impudently barged in without even acknowledging the prince.

I turned around, and, sure enough, it was exactly who I'd expected—Sirius Ulysses, a gray-haired, silver-eyed, youthful twenty-nine-year-old man and the captain of my Royal Guard. Sirius had a beautiful face that was simply out of this world... though it was tragically spoiled by his terrible manners. If he didn't speak, he'd be perfect.

Sirius angrily marched into the room, grabbed my arm, and straightened my back that was still bent from bowing.

Ack. Sorry. I turned around with my back still bent over in apology. That must have looked weird. Forgive me for showing you such an unseemly sight, I immediately thought, frightened by his disgruntled countenance.

"Hey, Vega, I get that you wanna dote on your little sister, but you mind wrapping things up and handing her over?" Sirius said, getting straight to the point without even a greeting. Normally, such behavior would be punished as an act of grave disrespect against royalty, but Sirius was born to a high-ranking noble family and was talented beyond belief. It helped, too, that my brothers—far above Sirius in terms of authority—let his behavior slide and even kissed up to him a bit, indirectly encouraging everyone else to look the other way too.

My brother Vega showed a brief look of shock at Sirius's sudden appearance but soon gathered himself and put on airs. "Well, if it isn't Master Sirius. What a lovely surprise. Unfortunately, as representative of the Supreme Council I have to interrogate my dear sister right now, although it does pain me to do so. Perhaps you haven't heard, but she shirked her duty to visit the Barbizet duchy. And would you believe it? She admits that she did so to go for a swim in Sutherland!"

*Hey, that's not...*quite *what I said!* I thought, but I reluctantly decided against speaking up. He was just too pleased with himself and ruining his mood would provoke him to strike back later many times over.

Sirius frowned at Vega's words. "Oh, perhaps *you* haven't heard," he said, mimicking the same aggravating tone of Vega's. My brother sensed something was off and stiffened. "The monster extermination demonstration in the Barbizet duchy went off without a hitch. The former first princess and Duchess of Barbizet herself took the role of saint in Serafina's stead, you see..." He paused there and walked to the front of Vega's desk, stepping onto the elevated floor and towering over Vega in his chair.

"Wh-what?" Vega stammered, confused. "M-Master Sirius...?"

Sirius spread his hands onto the desk, leaned forward, and stared at Vega from up close. "Four blue dragons appeared at the demonstration, but they were all defeated without a single casualty. Everybody was deeply impressed by the power of the duchess." He narrowed his eyes slightly and spoke in a whisper. "The only reason the Great Saint was to be dispatched to the Barbizet duchy at all was because *supposedly* no one but the Great Saint could handle such a demonstration."

Vega immediately understood where this was going. He went pale.

Sirius didn't let up one bit, tilting his head ever-so slightly before continuing. "Now, if the duchess was in fact capable of doing the demonstration all along, then the decision to send the Great Saint was a mistake from the start. The duchess should've been the go-to choice, as it'd let everybody know that her territory was in capable hands."

"M-Master Sirius..."

"'Course, it would be a big old problem if the Supreme Council made a mistake, yeah? Its authority would plummet. Why don't you hurry along and have another little meeting with that Council you're so proud of? Figure out where the blame lies. And once you're done with that, you can *do your damn job as Council representative and apologize to the Great Saint!* Apologize for almost robbing the Kingdom's most sacred, most priceless asset of five days' worth of time! Then you can show your gratitude for her fixing your idiot mistake by ignoring it completely!"

Sirius straightened back up and stared at Vega with cold eyes. Vega was a trembling mess at this point, and understandably so— Sirius was downright terrifying when he threatened someone. It didn't help that he also had an incredibly toned body from training every day. In fact, he was the strongest swordsman in the Kingdom.

Turning on his heel, Sirius began pacing toward me. He stopped in front of me and reached a hand to my cheek. "You're pale." He gently brushed his thumb against my face. "Serafina's skin is this pale," he muttered, "and yet you believed her words about going for a swim?"

"Th-that's..." stammered Vega.

"Vega, you're still green. Green enough to take Serafina's words at face value when she was trying to cover your sorry behinds—you and the rest of the Council. You didn't even consider the possibility that Serafina realized an error in the Council's decision and acted on her own authority to fix it! You may be the first prince, but you seem utterly incapable of seeing beyond the surface of things. If you keep that up, I doubt you'll last more than another minute here in the Royal Castle, what with all the scheming that goes on in these halls." Sirius spoke eloquently, but his words took on an unmistakable mocking tone toward the end.

Knowing full well that Sirius was mocking him, Vega blushed and bit his lip.

That's going too far, I thought as I looked up at Sirius. But he stood unrepentant, his expression unfazed in the slightest. I let out a weary sigh. *Oh, I get it now. He planned this all from the start.*

This was Sirius we were talking about, after all. There was no way he didn't figure out the real reason I went to Sutherland. Even so, he cooked up a story about it all being an effort on my part to save face for the Supreme Council, leaving no room for argument, and then mocked Vega to boot.

Ah jeez... Knowing my pigheaded brother, he was surely going to get back at me for this. Something to look forward to, I supposed.

I sighed again. Sirius pretended not to notice my distress and wordlessly put a hand on my back, then began pushing me toward the door.

"W-well, I guess we'll take our leave here, dear brother!" I said. Sirius was leaving without a word, rude as always, so I made doubly sure to say something in parting. My brother glared back at me, looking as though every second spent in my presence caused him unbearable rage, so I quickly made for the door.

Sirius said nothing even once we were out in the corridor. He simply stared straight ahead, undoubtedly furious, but matching my slow pace nonetheless. No matter how cross he got, he always had me in mind. It was funny, really. Everybody knew that he was the strongest, but very few knew the kindness within him.

After walking in silence for a while, I glanced up at his shapely face. "I'm back, Sirius," I whispered. "I'm sorry I didn't come see you first."

His feet came to a sudden halt, and he glared at me. "Call for me whenever something happens, Serafina. Even something as mundane as dealing with Vega's snideness. I'll come running for you. I always will."

I smiled. He was a big guy but a total worrywart at heart. "My, it's like I have another personal knight," I teased, spinning around to look at Canopus.

Sirius nodded. "Our roles are one and the same, as I am the captain of your Royal Guard." He then roughly tousled my hair. The familiar action seemed to calm him down as he put on a deeply sarcastic smile. "Heh. I can tell you held nothing back this time. Your hair is in such a mess, I doubt anyone would believe you were a princess."

I blushed bright red. "Wh—Sirius! You can't say such a thing to a lady!"

"A lady?" he laughed. "No, you're the same brat as ever."

Appalled by his rudeness, I protested with all my might.

"Why, I never! How could you say such a thing to a sixteen-year-old grown woman!"

It wasn't until later that I found out Sirius was the reason that the monster extermination demonstration in the Barbizet duchy went so well. The moment he heard I was going to Sutherland, he weighed the difference in strength between me and the Duchess of Barbizet and took a group of talented knights, the Royal Red Shield—which he'd trained himself—to the Barbizet duchy to make up for that difference. With them, the blue dragons were no hassle at all.

When I did later find out about this, I could only groan. "Grr, that darn Sirius!"

He was always, *always* perfect, never showing any weaknesses and always making the right decisions. What was more, he never bragged about his accomplishments. I would've never known what he did if I didn't find out from other people.

"Ugh, it's his fault I can't find a single lover," I muttered with a sigh.

That day, a letter with adela flowers pressed onto the paper arrived from the children of Sutherland. The moment I laid eyes on it, I broke into a smile.

Ah, right... It should take around ten years for the adela tree I planted to grow some flowers. When that time finally rolls around, I'll visit Sutherland again. I think next time, I'll bring my worrywart Royal Guard captain along with me too.

So I thought as I gazed at the beautiful deep-red petals of the adela flowers...

A Tale of the
Secret
Saint

The Demonstration in the Barbizet Duchy

(THREE HUNDRED YEARS AGO)

T HE MANSION OF THE Barbizet house was in uproar. Not a single hand was free—all were scrambling to prepare, for the Great Saint had abruptly canceled her appearance in the monster extermination demonstration that had been planned one year in advance.

All of the Barbizet duchy were astonished when the meager escort—four knights protecting a coach!—arrived. To their still greater astonishment, only a few sorry-looking ladies-in-waiting disembarked. The only one who seemed unfazed by this all was the former first princess and current duchess of Barbizet, the princess Shaula.

Shaula was a young and beautiful woman in her early twenties with green eyes and dark-red hair that came down to her shoulders. She looked at the ladies-in-waiting with trepidation before taking the letter and gift they offered.

After examining them, she burst into laughter. "I can't believe that girl actually pulled off such a trick, and right under the noses of those arrogant fools of the Royal Castle too! Oh...but does that mean she intends to make a round trip to and from Sutherland in just five days?"

She tilted her head curiously and looked at the four knights. Perhaps because she was formerly royalty, such a trivial gesture was enough to make them feel pressured. The knights averted their eyes uncomfortably, but that only served as an answer for Shaula.

She giggled. "I see, I see... so I'm going to have to do the monster extermination demonstration in place of Serafina, eh?"

She took the letter that the ladies-in-waiting offered and turned on her heel, briskly making her way to the parlor room. The duke hurried after her. Once inside, she took a seat on her favorite sofa right by the window and began happily reading the letter. Dubhe—the duke of Barbizet and her husband—peered through the door crack and watched her, his face lined with worry.

Dubhe was among the most powerful nobles in the Kingdom and possessed an appearance as frightening as a bear. That being said, the one who held the reins to the household was his wife, a woman over a decade younger than him. It was a common occurrence to see him nervously objecting to his wife's decisions.

"Shaula...is it not a little dangerous for you to replace Her Holiness?" he asked gingerly. His concern was warranted. The target of the monster extermination was a dangerous blue dragon nest located in a forest on their territory. The blue dragons had migrated to a cave within the duchy after losing their previous nest elsewhere. Blue dragons were S-rank monsters, so the sooner they were out of the duchy, the better. Unfortunately, it was considered far too dangerous to try and fight them without the Great Saint, and the matter had been put on hold for an entire year.

But on the long-awaited day of her arrival, the Great Saint was nowhere to be found. The mansion was understandably in a state of great panic.

Even with that panic, Dubhe kept his wits about him and spoke as calmly as he could. "Listen, Shaula. You may have fought against a lone S-rank monster before, but this time you'll be going into a nest full of an unknown number of blue dragons. Speaking as your husband, I can't permit you to put your life in such danger."

In contrast to her deathly serious husband, Shaula wore an amused smile. "But in her letter, Serafina personally asked me to replace her. Her intuition about this sort of thing—combat and the like—has never been wrong before. Yes, I'm certain I can do this. Heh heh...maybe this is my opportunity to grow even stronger as a saint!"

Though she spoke teasingly to lighten the mood, Dubhe remained uneasy. "N-no, Shaula, you mustn't!" he pleaded. "You're a wonderful saint, truly, but this blue dragon hunt is simply too dangerous! Just the thought of you attempting such a thing would keep me up at night!" His face grew paler by the second.

Shaula ignored him and rummaged through Serafina's gift. "Oh, look, it's the royal chef's handmade apple pie! How thoughtful of them." She slid the pie over to a maid. "Cut out a slice for me. I'd like to eat right away."

"Shaula!" Dubhe begged.

She received a cup of colorful black tea from a maid and inhaled its fragrance in an exaggerated manner, took a long, slow sip, and finally looked at her husband. "Ha ha! I'm sure it'll be fine. We even have some knights sent from the Royal Castle."

"But they only sent *four* knights! Distinguished as they are in their red uniforms, there's only so much that four knights can do. Even joined with our own duchy's knights, we're nowhere near strong enough!"

"For now, yes. But I'm sure more will arrive before we begin tomorrow afternoon."

"What do you..." he began, but a sudden clamor cut him off; just outside the mansion, the knights had begun to cheer loudly. Dubhe jolted up from his seat. "Wh-what's going on?!"

Shaula, on the other hand, only seemed mildly surprised. "He's here already? Goodness, his information network and ability to mobilize are unlike any other."

No sooner had her words finished than the door flew open to reveal a frightened butler. Behind the usually mild-mannered butler stood tens of red-uniformed knights.

Dubhe gasped. The only knights that wore red uniforms were the guardians of the Great Saint, the Royal Red Shield. Their brilliant gold-embroidered red uniforms held the admiration of the entire kingdom, and they were easily the strongest, most famous, and most respected group of knights in the kingdom, despite numbering less than a hundred.

But standing in the center of that prestigious group now was a man of still greater renown: Sirius Ulysses, the gray-haired and silver-eyed captain of the Royal Guard.

Sirius looked flatly at the stunned duke. The utter lack of emotion he showed kept all the would-be admirers of his beauty at a distance, as though he were drawing a line in the sand and forcing them to appreciate him only as an unreachable, solitary star in the sky. "It's been a while, Your Graces," he said. He never spoke more than the bare minimum with his clear, stoic voice. "The Royal Red Shield and I will assist you with tomorrow's monster extermination."

Debhe hemmed and hawed for a moment, bewildered by Sirius's statement. Eventually, he found his voice. "U-um, y-you mean to say you'll be partaking as well, Lord Ulysses?!" His surprise was understandable—it was a well-known fact that Sirius never fought unless the Great Saint commanded it.

Disregarding her surprised husband and seemingly unfazed by Sirius, Shaula picked up her cup of black tea. "Indeed, Master Sirius, it *has* been quite a while. Please, have a seat. Would you care for some of our family's proud apricot tea?"

But Sirius didn't move an inch.

Shaula sighed. "Without Serafina around, you're really nothing but a handsome doll. No sense of autonomy, you know? It's nothing but duty with you. Can't you enjoy yourself? Or do you believe that your Great Saint is so petty that she'd grow angry at you for sharing a cup of tea?"

"Sh-Shaula?!" Debhe fretted, surprised by his wife's rudeness. But Sirius and Shaula paid him no mind, simply staring one another down.

The first to avert their gaze was Sirius. The moment he did—in one flowing motion and without hesitation—he drew his sword and drove it into his right shoulder deep enough for the tip to protrude out his back.

"L-L-L-Lord Ulysses!" Debhe shrieked.

Sirius ignored Debhe and pulled his sword out of his shoulder with the same hand. "Can you heal this?" he asked in the same relaxed tone as one asking their neighbor for a cup of sugar. Blood spurted out of the wound.

With a serious look on her face, Shaula stood up and looked toward the ceiling. "My dear loving spirits! Come lend me your aid!"

In the blink of an eye, a woman appeared beside her. The woman looked almost human, save for the green skin that marked her as a spirit...and the fact that she floated a few inches off the ground. Her eyes were clear as emeralds, her hair green and shoulder-length, and she wore a simple white cloth coiled tightly around her body.

The spirit nodded respectfully to Shaula.

"Thank you for coming," said the saint. Then Shaula turned back to Sirius and put both of her hands over his wound. The spirit smiled and put her own hands over those of Shaula.

"Oh, benevolent spirit," Shaula chanted, "lend me your power. Stop this blood and seal this wound! *Heal Wound!*"

Light began to pour from Shaula's hands and into Sirius's shoulder. After mere seconds, she moved her hands away to reveal that the bleeding had stopped. The spirit then gave Shaula an inquiring look. Shaula thanked her and gave her a nod. With a smile, the spirit vanished just as suddenly as she'd appeared.

Sirius watched everything unfold without a word. He didn't even look down at his shoulder until the spirit left. Blood still covered his shoulder, making it hard to examine. He tried moving his right arm around.

Yes, it was surely healed. Sirius gave a satisfied nod. "Not bad." He turned to face Shaula and continued. "I see you haven't let your marriage keep you from practicing. You should be strong enough to handle the blue dragons. Based on reports, I predict we'll be facing somewhere around four or five blue dragons tomorrow. Make sure you rest well tonight."

Saying nothing further, Sirius turned on his heel and left the room, quickly followed by the red-uniformed knights. Their black mantles swayed as they moved, and the striking contrast of red and black burned into the minds of all who witnessed them.

Shaula and Dubhe shared a look and sighed deeply.

"Oh, Dubhe! Just what is *with* that man? He may be the Kingdom's strongest swordsman, but...well, he's as cold and eerie as ever, I suppose. He didn't so much as flinch when he thrust that sword into his own shoulder. Why, if he'd teared up or showed any signs of pain at all, he would've at least seemed human..."

"I doubt anyone will ever see Lord Ulysses cry," said Dubhe. "Or rather, I wouldn't in a million years ever *wish* to see him cry. No telling what he'd do to me if I witnessed it. Regardless, he more than lives up to the rumors about him. I can't believe he stabbed himself just to test your saint powers. No sane person would attempt that, even if they knew they would be healed." Such cowardly words were odd to hear from a man with such a bear-like physique, but Shaula didn't disagree.

Her shoulders sank in exhaustion. "I agree, no sane person would even imagine such a method. Even the knights behind him looked shocked beyond belief. But your read on the situation is a little off—he wasn't testing my saint powers. He wanted to test my ability to respond to unforeseen situations. He used his own body to ascertain whether I could act without falling into a panic."

He shook his head. "Well...I'm glad I chose not to join the Royal Red Shield."

The two shared another look and sighed deeply once again.

The following day was blessed with clear weather.

The expedition made their way through the forest toward the blue dragon nest. The group consisted of Shaula and Debhe, thirty knights of the Royal Red Shield, thirty knights of the duchy, a group of saints for support, and a number of coaches transporting the nobles who came to observe.

Before long, the cave that the blue dragons had chosen for their nest was visible in the distance. The nobles stopped and hid at a rocky outcrop where they could safely watch the battle unfold. The knights from the duchy and the saints that had come for support—all under the command of Debhe—spread out to protect the nobles while Shaula and the Royal Red Shield continued to advance.

But the moment the group left the rocky outcrop and came

into plain view, a blue dragon guarding the entrance to the cave spotted them and let out a fierce cry.

"Graoooooah!"

Blue dragons crawled from the narrow cave, one by one. The group could've attacked then and there, leaving no room for the blue dragons to fight but instead Sirius waited for them to all come out—perhaps out of consideration for the spectating nobles.

The knights formed a tight half circle around the cave entrance, with Sirius at the center of the formation. Shaula positioned herself around ten meters behind him. Her healing magic had a range of about fifteen meters, so some knights were out of her range, but this was the closest she could reasonably come to the blue dragons. A spirit floated beside her, smiling brightly.

Three dragons appeared after the lookout's call, and now four dragons faced the knights. The terrifying beasts towered over their surroundings, each nearly five meters tall.

The instant the last dragon had completely left the cave, Sirius drew his sword and brandished it skyward. Sunlight streamed from the clear sky, and the blade shone with light. With both hands, he spun the blade in a brilliant, gleaming arc.

"The heavens and earth revolve and flow their strength into me. *Total Body Strengthening.*" Space seemed to warp around him the moment those words left his lips. He appeared to change; his very presence seemed weightier, denser—an odd distortion that could've left any viewer wondering if they were seeing an illusion.

At the same time, the mages finished preparing their attack magic. Blue dragons were weak against flame, so they all cast fire magic.

"*Conflagrate!*"

"*Flame Bullets!*"

"*Chain of Flame!*"

Each of the spells were advanced level. They spiraled together in a brilliant, red blaze and coiled around their targets. The blue dragons, being S-rank monsters, couldn't be fatally wounded by such magic, but it was enough to make them instinctively sink back and roar with pain.

When the flames enveloped the dragons, the twenty-or-so knights made their move with Sirius at the front. He walked unhurriedly, but his weight seemed to increase with each step he made across the earth. Once he was directly in front of the nearest blue dragon, it swiped at him with its claws and bit at him with its gaping maw.

He dodged both attacks with ease. Then, using his momentum from dodging, he fluidly shifted into a horizontal slash at the dragon's leg, sinking half the length of his blade into dragon flesh. Dragon scales were said to be impenetrable, yet his sword somehow broke through the scales like they were paper. He pulled his sword out, and chipped scales flaked off of the blade. The knights positioned behind Sirius then dove their swords into the opening.

"Graaaaaaooh!" The blue dragon let out an agonized cry as yet another barrage of fire magic enclosed it.

Sirius took advantage of the blue dragon's faltering posture and leaped up to the underside of its chin, where its inverted dragon scale—the only vulnerable scale on a dragon that grew in reverse—was located. He poured all his strength into his arms and plunged his sword into the dragon's weak spot, but it didn't seem like his effort mattered in the end—the blade slid in like a hot knife through butter.

"Graaaaaagh!" As Sirius pulled out his blade, the blue dragon commenced its death throes and then fell to the ground with a deafening thud. The ground shook, kicking a cloud of dust up over the dead dragon.

Sirius began moving toward another dragon, the other knights following close behind. None of them so much as hesitated in the face of multiple S-rank monsters—the mark of men led by a powerful and reliable commander.

The group went on to defeat the remaining three dragons in the same manner as the first. A few knights suffered broken bones from the whip of a dragon's tail or cuts from their claws and fangs, but Shaula was able to heal them quickly enough that they could immediately rejoin the fray.

After the last dragon fell to the ground with a thundering slam, the knights flicked the blood from their blades and sheathed their weapons. The battle was over. The knights rejoiced, now heroes who had vanquished the atrocious monsters that had threatened the area for a year. But Sirius, in the center of the group, remained expressionless. It was as though he thought nothing of the whole matter.

The knights and Shaula were met with cheers and applause as they returned to the watching nobles. The nobles showered them in praise, especially Shaula, saying the territory was in good hands with a saint powerful enough to solo heal in a battle against blue dragons.

To such praise, she muttered, "I can't say I did all that much. The knights were simply far and away more powerful..." Unfortunately, her words were taken as mere modesty, earning her even more respect.

That night, a banquet was held to allow the knights and the nobles to mingle. But as Shaula had predicted, Sirius and his knights were absent. They'd already left to return to the Royal Castle.

The people of the Barbizet duchy and the nobles of the neighboring territories sang the praises of Sirius and his knights—as well as the praises of Shaula.

"Such a brilliant group of knights! They neither boast of their deeds nor allow themselves to indulge in pleasures!"

"And they're led by Captain Sirius too! He's so strong and handsome... He's the perfect knight!"

With the blue dragon extermination a clear, resounding success, everyone had nothing but praise for the strength of the Royal Guard and the brilliance of the Duchess of Barbizet.

After a merry, boisterous night, the banquet ended in high spirits.

Then, after four weeks passed and the excitement died down somewhat, a large package arrived for the Barbizet couple. Inside, they found a rug of shocking beauty and a concise note from the sender, Sirius Ulysses:

To replace the rug I dirtied.

"Come to think of it," Shaula mused, "Master Sirius did stain a rug when he hurt himself in our parlor room. The blue dragon extermination overshadowed the whole thing, so I completely forgot about it, but I believe our splendid maids already cleaned the blood out of it. Regardless...this rug he sent us must be worth several times more than the one he bled on, isn't it?"

"At the very least," Debhe responded. "I must say, he's certainly a man who can stand with the elites of the Royal Castle. How incredibly considerate!"

"It's a bit much, though. He's certainly more sensible and generous than his curtness led me to believe, but there was no need for him to show us *this* much consideration. He's already done enough for us by defeating those blue dragons in our duchy. If anything, we're the ones who should be thanking him..." She trailed off, deep in thought. Eventually, she looked up with an impish grin on her face.

Debhe knew that grin. It rarely boded well. "Sh-Shaula..." he pleaded, "'whatever you're thinking, please reconsid—"

"I shall set off for the Royal Castle tomorrow," she said gravely, and that was that.

It was clear to Debhe that his wife was planning to do something at the Royal Castle, and he could only hope against hope that it was something good.

Whether or not his prayers were heard, one thing was certain: In that moment, Shaula genuinely intended to repay Sirius for the favor of slaying those blue dragons.

A Tale of the
Secret
Saint

Blue Sapphire, Prince of the Arteaga Empire

"FIA..." I murmured, lost in my own elation, "I, Blue Sapphire, have at last returned to your kingdom."

It was largely coincidence that brought me back to this country, starting with the Grand Chamberlain's recommendation that we investigate Náv for traces of Fia, the Goddess of Creation. I used to only think of our Grand Chamberlain as a nagging, wrinkly old geezer, but his suggestion moved me so much that—for the first time—I felt some fondness toward him. That fondness vanished soon enough, though, when he harshly shot down my offer to participate in the investigation. Still, I had the last laugh, because I was able to sneak into the investigation team without his knowledge.

The investigation team was led by our empire's proud knight brigade commander, Cesare Rubino. He was a loyal man in his early fifties who towered nearly two meters high, and he boasted a long record of heroic feats. His face was rugged like a boulder, and he only ever spoke the bare minimum. At first, he seemed quite intimidating, but he was actually a kind man, much adored by his subordinates. I knew this for a fact, as he'd noticed my attempt to slip into the investigation team on the day we set out for Náv...and he chose to look the other way. Bless his heart.

In the end though, it didn't matter much, as Red Ruby came to see the team off—even though it was supposed to be a covert mission—and he pointed me out immediately.

"Blue Sapphire!" he shouted. "Why are you trying to sneak in on this alone! That's not fair!"

What a childish thing to say. If he thought about it for a moment, he'd realize that he—the bearer of the crown—could never take part in a covert mission like this. It was only sensible that I go instead.

Endless whining about how unfair it was that I got to go was simply immature. He could stand to learn a thing or two about how a leader comports himself from Cesare. Still, voicing such thoughts would only lead to more trouble, so I merely lowered my gaze and kept quiet.

The usually taciturn Cesare then stepped in and whispered something in a low voice to my brother. After one last groan, Red Ruby finally fell silent.

Our departure was met with perfect weather. I felt as though the cloudless skies reflected the state of my bright, hopeful heart. Yes, we'd surely find the miracle-bringing Goddess in no time at all.

We began by disguising ourselves as adventurers and searching the forest where my brothers and I met Fia. I admired the scenery fondly, nostalgic for those magical moments with her, but we encountered only atrocious monsters. Not a single clue to Fia's whereabouts could be found in the forest.

Our next visit was to the adventurers' guild, but that also proved fruitless. Even expanding the breadth of our investigation to the neighboring towns and forests yielded no results.

Faced with the futility of our search, I slumped my shoulders, all too late realizing the true purpose of the Grand Chamberlain's proposal: That sly fox knew full well that we would fail to find Fia. He wanted us to exhaust ourselves in the search so that we would finally get over our obsession with her and seek out other women.

Of course, that was all a misunderstanding on the Grand Chamberlain's part. Fia wasn't even of age. Though I couldn't prove it, I suspected that it was a purposeful choice on behalf of the Goddess: Taking on such a young form prevented others from having unpardonable thoughts toward her. The feelings I held toward Fia were obviously not romantic, and, by extension, my lack of interest in other women wasn't tied to Fia.

More than a month had passed now, since we arrived in the Náv Kingdom. I sat down next to Cesare in the dining hall of the inn and sighed heavily.

"Is something the matter, my liege?" he asked.

"No. I was just thinking that things are going exactly the way that cunning devil back at the castle planned. We'll probably have to call it quits sooner or later and return home empty-handed, just like he wants."

I was speaking of my distaste for the Grand Chamberlain, but Cesare seemed to feel it was criticism toward himself. "I am deeply sorry. Even with a month of time and a hundred knights, I have failed to find you a single clue. Please forgive me for my incompetence." He sat with his back straight and lowered his head.

Rather troubled by such sincerity, I replied, "No, no—you haven't done anything wrong at all. We should've never sent a man of your importance on what amounts to an errand for the emperor in the first place. Don't worry about it all that much." I took a small roasted bean the size of my fingernail and flung it into my mouth, then checked to see if Cesare had relaxed.

That overly serious hulk of a man just shook his head. "No. I owe the Emperor much for allowing me to keep my role when he took the throne, and yet I haven't done anything to repay him in the three months he's ruled."

"Hmm. But isn't that a good thing? After all, no work means that his rule has been peaceful, despite the sudden shift in power. C'mon, eat some beans." A bit baffled by Cesare's earnest stubbornness, I rested my chin on my hands.

Come to think of it, at the meeting when Red Ruby informally announced his decision to keep Cesare on as knight brigade commander, a meeting that I attended along with Green Emerald, Cesare had said something similar...

"Your Imperial Majesty and Your Imperial Highnesses, I thank you from the bottom of my heart for allowing me to retain the position of commander. I know full well it is standard for civil and military positions to be reformed when a new emperor takes the throne. As such,

I assumed that as head military officer, I would be replaced. While I am not too attached to my own position, I was concerned about what might happen to the knights who serve under me, were I to leave."

I remembered thinking it impressive how talkative and open he was about his thoughts, but I later learned that he was usually quite a bit more taciturn. He'd been pushing himself to speak, perhaps, or maybe he was only talkative when it came to thanking his lord or helping his subordinates?

I pondered such things as I gazed at him. Suddenly, he met my eyes. "Regardless, I have Master Blue and your brothers, the three leaders of our country, to thank for allowing me to retain my position."

Red Ruby, my oldest brother and the emperor, respected the opinions of his brothers and chose to have us rule as a trio, granting both of us the authority to make decisions as well. In a sense, Cesare's current position was indeed thanks to all three of us...but when you got down to it, he was simply the right man for the job. All of this gratitude was unnecessary.

"You're kinda stiff, you know that? Drop the formalities a bit. I'm trying to go by just 'Blue' to fit in with the townspeople here, but people will realize what's up if you keep calling me 'Master Blue' this and 'Master Blue' that."

Back at the start of our mission, I asked him to treat me like any other subordinate in order to hide my identity, but it seems like he just couldn't bring himself to be that casual.

"You know," I added, "Fia is the one you should really be thanking, if you think about it. Until we visited this land half a year ago, my brothers and I were nobodies." I suddenly felt the urge to talk about Fia, perhaps to convey to him why my brothers and I were so desperate to find her. "I'm sure you know, but my brothers and I were kept away from the main family and lived with distant relatives since birth. Nobody expected anything from us, and nobody visited us. My older brothers were fated to one day die from their curse. And when they were no longer around to shield us, my sister and I would have surely been next on the chopping block. I was certain we would all die without achieving anything."

It sounded like I was talking about some far-off past, but it was our reality mere months ago. I genuinely believed we all would've died if we hadn't met Fia.

"Have you ever imagined what my brothers' curses must have been like?" I said, shaking my head at the very thought. "Constantly enduring the pain of bleeding from their foreheads, never having enough blood to move their bodies as they willed, their minds permanently fogged by blood loss. That was their whole life. Yet they never once complained and always reassured me that they'd figure something out. I, with my weak constitution, was told I wouldn't even grow to adulthood. They always protected me, though, and I thought I would be happy if I could simply one day die for their sakes."

I took up my glass of alcohol and slowly drank it dry. For a time, we sat in silence. "Fia is *truly* a Goddess," I said finally. "She listened to the story of us nobodies, sympathized with us, and encouraged us. Only after all that did she remove our curses. Do you understand what I'm saying? She didn't remove our curses as soon as we met. No, she waited until she *knew* us before removing them."

I closed my eyes and thought back to our time together. "She was testing us to see if we were worthy of salvation, worthy of the power and duty she would give us. And she deemed us worthy. That's why my brothers and I are so driven. We want to prove that she chose the right people to thank her for giving us a chance when nobody else had."

I still couldn't describe how moved I felt when she gave us our duty and the power we needed to fulfill it. That moment changed our lives forever.

"Cesare, I genuinely believe you are the right man for the position of knight commander. But the true reason you weren't replaced is because Fia taught me and my brothers to believe in people. Of course, the three of us would be long dead if it weren't for Fia, but surely you understand what I mean." I looked Cesare squarely in the eyes now. "All of this is thanks to Fia. We owe our lives to her."

He was quiet for some time, but then he balled his hands into fists. "Master Blue, I swear I will find your Goddess," he declared.

"I see," I said, smiling happily—he understood at last. "I'm counting on you."

One week later, a stroke of luck led us to the Ruud knight family. We heard that a daughter of the Ruud family had red hair and golden eyes and rejoiced, but upon further listening, we learned she was actually already of age. Still, we had no other leads, so we decided to pay them a visit.

Being a knight family, it made more sense they would welcome other knights in, so we did away with our disguises and donned our knight gear. We made up some story about being under the employ of an Arteagian noble and traveling to some earldom on Náv's borders for an errand. Oddly enough, they accepted the story without any questions whatsoever. I thought it strange that they could be so careless, but perhaps the lord was a bit of a lax man.

"Oh, a red-haired girl? Yes, that'd be the second daughter, Fia." Here we were, with no expectation of success, and the Ruud family knight said those explosive words in such a casual tone.

"Wha—guh—?" The words stuck in my throat. "D-did you just say *Fia*?!"

The knight looked at me oddly and pointed up at a family portrait hanging above the fireplace. "Um, yes. She has a fairly common name, but her hair is really quite something. You can see her up there."

It was only several steps away, but I ran forward and grabbed the portrait. Sure enough, it depicted Fia—the very Goddess I owed my life to—alongside what looked like her family.

"F-Fia!" I fell to my knees, as if struck by lightning. Surprised, Cesare ran to me, but all I could manage to do was point at the portrait with a trembling hand. "C-Cesare! It's Fia!"

He silently took the portrait from my hands and stared at the image of Fia.

"Are you two acquaintances of hers?" the knight asked.

"Because she left for the royal capital to become a knight the instant she came of age."

"She's of age?!" I exclaimed. "What?! How?! I-Is the age of adulthood in Náv ten or something?!"

"No, it's fifteen. Lady Fia is a bit lacking in height—and a few other areas—but she is a full-fledged adult."

"I...I-I c-can't believe it. She's an adult with that kind of body? No, perhaps that body is simply the form that the Goddess wishes to spend her immortal life in?!"

Thinking that a bout of madness had overtaken me, the knight took pity on me and kindly seated me in a chair. He then fetched me something warm to drink. I sipped from my cup to calm myself down as the knight pointed out the strange, unintelligible objects by the fireplace.

"That abstract piece of art there was handmade by Lady Fia. It's made from a broken sword and is meant to signify victory. It was made to commemorate her thousandth practice match loss. And over there is..."

The unintelligible piece of "art" made from wood and a broken sword suddenly took on the splendor of a national-treasure-class wonder to me.

"The eldest daughter, Lady Oria, dotes on Lady Fia a lot," the knight said, "so she's kept this collection of things related to Lady Fia as mementos."

I gasped. "Oh...how wonderful! That Lady Oria is truly a genius!" I praised and praised the eldest daughter until my breath ran ragged.

Take that, Grand Chamberlain! You always scolded me for having no kind words for the ladies, but I just hadn't discovered any worth my praise until now!

As I continued to appreciate Fia's superb and unusual works of art, Cesare spoke to the knight from behind me. "Sir, I know we've imposed on you enough already, but would it be at all possible to acquire a portrait of Miss Fia? The lord I serve is in search of a fiancée. He mentioned that the daughter of a Náv Kingdom knight family would be ideal." Cesare drew his sword from its pitch-black scabbard and offered it as a sign of his word.

The blade used to belong to the Black Knight, said to be the strongest swordsman in history. It was at the very least a national-treasure-class item. To offer such a sword in exchange for a portrait of the divine Fia...it was a fair trade indeed!

I felt admiration for Cesare's resolute decision and told myself I would have to give him the greatest sword in our treasury to replace his own once we returned to the Empire. But before that...

"C-Cesare! That lord you mentioned wasn't me, was it?!" I stammered, suddenly at a loss for words. "F-Fia...as my fiancée?!"

But Cesare seemed disinterested in talks of engagement. Instead, he handed me the portrait of Fia he'd received in exchange for his national-treasure-class sword. The picture was small enough to hold with one hand and featured Fia in a blue dress that was more elaborate than the ones I saw on the village girls of the area.

"Ah, sh-she's wearing my color!" I exclaimed, overwhelmed with excitement.

Cesare silently nodded. Looking back on it now, he probably intentionally picked out a portrait with her in a blue dress, but I was too overjoyed to even consider that.

"F-Fia is still with us!" I cried. "That means there's something she's still trying to achieve in this world! I'll...I'll go help her! We're heading to the royal capital!" I proudly declared. Cesare stayed silent, his head bowed. He'd predicted I would say such a thing.

My brothers and the Grand Chamberlain had given us two months' time. Taking into account the number of days it would take to return to the Empire, we would likely go over our allotted time...but such quibbles were immaterial.

Spirit renewed, I prepared to head for the royal capital...and to Fia!

A Tale of the Secret Saint

Commandant Desmond Receives a Report Regarding Fia, Again

"COMMANDANT, I have an urgent report to make!"

My subordinate rushed into the room with a deathly serious look on their face, but I noticed that the corners of their mouth were breaking into a smile. Whatever they had to report was probably something I wouldn't like...probably something incredibly urgent and important, potentially even world-shaking.

But it would surely be too ludicrous to take seriously. "And who, exactly, does it involve?" I asked.

"Fia Ruud of the First Knight Brigade, Sir!"

"Damnit! Not her again!" Still sitting in my chair, I kicked the desk in front of me. "Ha ha ha! Just how much of my time is she going to rob from me?! All the reports concerning her are utterly outlandish and incomprehensible, and yet every one of them remains urgent, important, and high-risk!"

I glared at my subordinate and shouted at them now. "So what is it this time?! Has Fia found a *second* familiar? Or maybe she's invented a new game to replace chess? Ha ha ha...ha...haaaa..."

My subordinate ignored my remarks and made their report without meeting my eyes. "According to an urgent report from Sutherland, Fia Ruud has been recognized as the Great Saint's reincarnation by the people of Sutherland. As a result—"

"Wait, what did you just say?!" Shocked, I stood to my feet. "Fia was *what*?!"

"Um...she has been recognized...as the Great Saint's reincarnation? And—"

"Ha ha ha ha ha ha! Incredible. Just *incredible*! The Great Saint's reincarnation! The great, sacred, and untouchable Great Saint! What a *divine* pain in my ass this'll be! Gaaah, damn it!"

In my anger, I grabbed a nearby open inkwell and threw it at the window. With a loud crack, the inkwell shattered the window and clattered down, down, down...

It actually broke the window?! Wonderful! Another mess I have to clean up!

The infuriating work just kept piling up. I glared at my subordinate. "Listen up, Zand! We need to send an emergency message to Cyril! As lord of Sutherland, he has a duty to manage his territory! But instead, he's just twiddling his thumbs as Fia gets mistaken for the Great Saint!"

"Sir? The report never said anything about the recognition of Fia Ruud as the Great Saint's reincarnation being an error."

"It's obviously an error! If someone like her can be the Great Saint's reincarnation, then I might as well be the reincarnation of the strongest swordsman in history! Look at me, everybody! I'm the Black Knight!"

I was about to complain more, but the door suddenly opened without so much as a knock. *Who'd be bold enough to enter my room without knocking?*

The door fully swung open to reveal...a black-haired knight who looked just like Zackary? No, that *was* Zackary. But why was half of his hair pitch-black? An absolutely *inky* black, even, as if...as...if...

Oops. *Oh, crap! This is bad. Really, really bad! What if the inkwell I threw landed on Zackary's head and now he's here?!*

I quickly turned to my subordinate. "Don't just stand there, Zand! If you're going to throw inkwells, you should damn well pick them up!"

Zand looked at me incredulously. I could only hope that one day they understood this was for the best. Zackary was lenient toward the mistakes of those under him but utterly merciless toward his colleagues' mistakes. *Please, Zand! I'll treat you to all the food and drink you want for a week! Just bear the shame for me this one time, eh?!*

But Zackary didn't fall for it. "That's an interesting joke, Desmond," he said roughly. "I came running here as soon as I was showered in ink... What an absurd combination of words, that! Showered in ink, ha! It sounds ridiculous, yet it actually happened. Look—half of my hair is dyed. It seems someone aimed an inkwell at my head. Sure surprised me. So, I ran the direction it was thrown from and found your room...with your subordinate Zand facing *away* from the window. In other words, Zand didn't have time to throw the inkwell, did they?"

"Ha...ha..." All I could manage was light laughter.

"Oh? Are you laughing, Desmond? Yes, I suppose this is somewhat funny. How could I allow myself to be hit by an inkwell? I should have just dodged it, no? Yes, I was taking an afternoon nap underneath a tree. And yes, I was completely asleep and defenseless, but a knight brigade captain like me should be capable of dodging such a thing, regardless. How shameful."

"N-not at all, Zackary! You're a wonderful man! A man among men! Even when drenched like this, your greatness shines through the ink! I mean it!" I frantically laid on the compliments, but the look on his face said it all: He thought I was mocking him.

He glanced toward Zand. "Zand, I'm sorry, but I need to talk to Desmond about something important. Could you give us some time alone?"

"N-no! Don't go! You can't leave me, Zand!" I pleaded, but they denied me with a cold gaze.

"Such compelling words, Captain," said Zand. "If only you'd used them on your ex-fiancée, then maybe you'd be married by now. But I'm just your subordinate, and so your words mean nothing to me."

"Wh-what?! That topic is taboo!" I groaned. "Don't dredge up my old wounds!"

Zand ignored me and spoke to Zackary with a serious look. "Understood, Captain Zackary. My working hours are over, so I'll be heading home now. Please, spend as much time as you need with Captain Desmond."

"Z-Zand, you're my closest confidant! How could you betray me?!"

"Oh, please. If you valued me that much, you wouldn't try to pin your actions on me. I'm no confidant, I'm just an ordinary knight, and it's precisely because I'm just an ordinary knight that I can leave you in this room with Captain Zackary and not feel an ounce of guilt."

"Z-Zand, no..." I pleaded. They simply smiled at me and left me alone with a wickedly smiling Zackary.

That day, I learned firsthand what it was like to be on the receiving end of one of Zackary's scoldings.

A Tale of the
Secret Saint

Canopus and His Heartbreak Party

(THREE HUNDRED YEARS AGO)

O N THE DAY I was appointed Serafina's personal knight, I didn't return to my room until very late.

I knew that being the personal knight of a princess was an important duty that would keep me incredibly busy. As such, I was more than fully prepared to undergo lengthy formalities and receive a long explanation of my duties on the very first day. What I never expected was for my time to be taken up, not by meaningful guidance, but by the endless prattling of officials.

"Oh, how terrible! How utterly terrible! In all the hundreds of years our grand kingdom has existed, never has a former islander been chosen as the personal knight of royalty! Canopus, you've ushered in a new era for the kingdom! A grim, grim era!"

"How could a commoner possibly be the personal knight of a princess?! And of all people, it's the second princess herself—endowed with such rare, beautiful red hair! Hmph! Do you even know what a mess you've made of things?!"

I stood silent as they repeated the same grievances ad nauseam. While I could've done without all the complaining, I at least felt as though they truly valued Serafina and only complained because they genuinely wanted the best possible candidate to be her personal knight. In essence, we all served and treasured the same Lady. I could see myself finding a way to work with them, in time.

Eventually, I was freed from their harassment and able to return to my room at the knight dorm, where the lights were already out. I quietly opened the door—it was late, and my room-mate was likely long asleep. I'd shut the door as silently as I could and sat down atop my bed, when suddenly the room blazed with light.

Blinded, I shielded my eyes...and half a dozen or so cheering knights grabbed hold of me. "Congratulations on getting rejected, Canopus!"

"Yeah, man, don't let it get to ya! Ain't no way a commoner rooming in a dorm was ever getting chosen to be a personal knight!"

"Don't feel so heartbroken, my guy! Her Highness is too much for a big ol' noodle like you to handle anyway! You can settle for just hanging with your pals tonight, eh? Drinking with the guys ain't bad!"

One after another, they began piling on top of me.

I suppose they hadn't heard that I *was* selected as the second princess's personal knight.

"Guh...g-get...off me!" Under all their weight, I could only muster up a feeble croak. Training every day made every one of them a bundle of raw muscle. There was nothing I could do to fight back against their collective weight.

After I hit the one on top without holding anything back, they relented and got off one by one, laughing all the while.

I panted heavily, trying to get as much oxygen as I could back into my body as I scanned the room. Half a dozen knights whom I knew well were crammed into the little dormitory, all of them wearing guileless smiles. They'd clearly been waiting for me in the darkness, even at this time of night, all so they could cheer me up. Upon closer inspection, I even noticed alcohol and snacks on a table in the corner.

I was grateful from the bottom of my heart, but... "Thank you all, but there is no need to console me. I was chosen as the personal knight of Her Highness the Second Princess."

"Er...what?"

"Your jokes are a bit hard to follow, my friend. Tell us what really happened, okay?"

Seeing such burly knights tilting their heads like confused children was amusing, but I refrained from laughter. "Exactly what I said. It seems that Her Highness discarded the personal knight that was originally chosen for her in favor of me. Starting today, I am officially the personal knight of Her Highness."

They gave me doubtful looks. Who could blame them? It had always been a long shot. The litany of criticisms I'd heard from officials today made clear they wished it'd been even longer.

I took the sword at my hip, sheath and all, and thrust it before me. "As proof I was appointed, I have this sword I got from the vice-commander."

Even in the dim dorm room, the intricate handle and decorative sheath were visible at a glance. Those with good sight could even make out an engraved rose, the symbol of the second princess. Still doubtful, the knights drew close to inspect the sword. Afterward, they let out a deep sigh.

"So, you're serious, then? Wow...we got a real lady killer here, huh? Who knew? Making even royalty fall for ya!"

"Huh...I'll admit you have some skill with the sword, but I hear those noble ladies all consider it vulgar to swing swords for a living. Just what methods did you stoop to, getting chosen like that?"

"Dude, hold up, this is impossible! Look, this info stays between us, but I heard that Sargas of the Aldridge Marquess family was pre-selected to be Her Highness's personal knight. Canopus, no offense, you ain't bad-looking, but Sargas is next level! If I were a princess, I'd choose the aristocratic dreamboat over some random looker from the sticks any day!"

"You guys..." I grumbled. They finally believed me, but instead of congratulations, I was getting roasted. I was about to complain when they all burst into laughter without warning.

"Ha ha ha! You're incredible, Canopus!"

"This is amazing! There have been tons of strong commoners loyal to the Kingdom, but none of 'em ever made it as far as you! This is a world first!"

"Well done, Canopus!"

One after another, they all praised me. Then they poured me a glass and encouraged me to down it. Stunned by their about-face, I blinked a few times in confusion...but at the sight of their smiling faces, I couldn't help but break out in a smile of my own.

I raised a glass with everyone and, filled with mirth, reflected on how lucky I was to be chosen. Then I raised a toast to Serafina, who had made such a wonderful night possible.

Regrettably, I drank too much and reeked of alcohol the entirety of the following day.

"Canopus smells kinda funny," Serafina muttered at one point, and I felt regret to the very depths of my heart.

It would take time, resolve, and considerably more self-restraint before I became worthy of being her personal knight.

A Tale of the
Secret Saint

Sargas of the Aldridge Marquess Family— A Worry-free Smile

MY NAME IS SARGAS, of the Aldridge Marquess family. As I was of noble birth and held the position of Second Knight Brigade Vice-Captain, I was unofficially offered the position of personal knight to Second Princess Serafina.

It was an important duty, one that promised a good future. It was common knowledge that the vice-commander, soon to be a commander, doted on the second princess. Becoming her personal knight all but guaranteed one would move up in the knight brigades.

I entered the great hall where the selection would be carried out in high spirits...only for Serafina to choose a completely different person as her personal knight. What was more, he was a commoner. Not even a mainlander but a man from a group of former islander peoples who were widely regarded as lesser.

Yes, lineage isn't the only thing necessary to receive such a high honor, but...I had truly believed that I was special merely because I was born "chosen". For that, I felt deeply ashamed of myself.

Several years later, I was approached by Sirius, the captain of Serafina's Royal Guard. "You've got quite some skill with the sword. Any interest in joining the Royal Red Shield?"

Being in the Royal Red Shield was the highest possible honor. "Please, allow me to serve and protect Her Highness," I said and performed the knight salute.

He nodded. It was enough.

The very next day, I was already in the red uniform of the Royal Red Shield and protecting Serafina up close. I thought the transition would take more time, as I was in a higher position than most who were assigned here, but I was transferred over without any hassle on my end whatsoever. Despite the doubtless mountains of paperwork involved, Sirius was clearly as talented at cutting through red tape as he was at cutting down monsters.

Several years thereafter, Canopus was granted the title of Blue Knight and I witnessed him being ordered to forgo his red uniform for a blue one. For some strange reason, I couldn't help but feel relieved. I realized then that I wasn't as at peace with losing my spot as Serafina's personal knight as I'd have liked to believe. Secretly, the snub had eaten away at me all these years. But then I saw Canopus in his blue uniform, looking deeply vexed about it, while I still wore the red that symbolized Serafina...and all my cares faded away.

Serafina seemed to find fault in the smile I'd unknowingly made. "My, Sargas," she said, rather grumpily. "I can't say I've seen you smile like that many times. Since I've been caged up in the castle for two days without a single fun thing to do, would you be so kind as to share some of your amusement with me?"

"Of course. I was just thinking I am truly blessed to be able to protect Your Highness." The moment I said those words, I once again felt keenly that it was true. While I might not have been chosen as her personal knight, I was able to join her Royal Guard and protect her. Belatedly, I realized I was truly blessed to be where I was.

"Hmm? Um, thank you...for protecting me...?" She tilted her head in confusion, my feelings failing to quite reach her.

Not many knights could serve the lord they wanted, and not many lords were an honor to serve...but the one looking at me so oddly now was both of these things, and that brought me true joy.

A Tale of the
Secret
Saint

Afterword

Hello, touya here. It's a pleasure to meet you again. Thank you for reading Volume 3 of *A Tale of the Secret Saint*.

I hope everyone's staying safe during the pandemic. I'm praying things settle down quickly, and we can all return to our everyday lives safe and sound.

We finally reached the stories from Three Hundred Years Ago with this volume. I was able to have my favorite scene illustrated for the cover, and what a beautiful illustration at that! I also really like the Fia x Cyril color illustration at the beginning. Thank you, Chibi!

On an unrelated note, I do Omikuji every year. Omikuji is this fortune telling thing in Japan where you draw a random fortune from a box on New Year's and have your luck for the year told. This year, for the first time in my life, I pulled "super bad luck." It exists, everyone! Despite what people say, you *can* actually pull super bad luck! A bit fearfully, I read the contents of the fortune and, I gotta say, things aren't looking good for me, folks. But at the end of the fortune, there was a little line that said, "You've hit rock bottom, now you can only go up!" That sure is some positive thinking! But I guess it's a genuine way of looking at things, isn't it? If things are at their worst, they can only get better! If we suppose I'm at the rock bottom of my life now—which isn't even all that bad—I must be living a good life.

Or...maybe my life's comparatively full of bad luck and I just don't realize it? Come to think of it, I *did* somehow slip on the stairs and fracture my tailbone a while back. Just sitting down proved a struggle for a while...and I never found those New Year's lottery cards I lost. I feel like they would have been big winners too...

Well, at least I'm still alive and kicking. Things can only go up from here!

I'd like to thank you for reading this far. I'd also like to thank everyone who made this book possible—it couldn't have been easy with the current pandemic going on. It's been a pleasure.